T0365915

The
LONG MAN

LIZZY LLOYD

authorHOUSE

AuthorHouse™ UK
1663 Liberty Drive
Bloomington, IN 47403 USA
www.authorhouse.co.uk
Phone: 0800.197.4150

Published by AuthorHouse 09/23/2016

ISBN: 978-1-5246-3548-0 (sc)
ISBN: 978-1-5246-3549-7 (e)

Print information available on the last page.

Any people depicted in stock imagery provided by Thinkstock are models, and such images are being used for illustrative purposes only. Certain stock imagery © Thinkstock.

This book is printed on acid-free paper.

Because of the dynamic nature of the Internet, any web addresses or links contained in this book may have changed since publication and may no longer be valid. The views expressed in this work are solely those of the author and do not necessarily reflect the views of the publisher, and the publisher hereby disclaims any responsibility for them.

CONTENTS

To all purists and historians – it's fiction!

CHAPTER 1

COLIN'S STORY

The marsh sang all around him; the cacophony of crickets, warblers, larks and bees drowned out the sounds of road and air traffic and the pounding in his head that was failure, misery and humiliation. The knees of his jeans soaked up the brown peat water and his hands, moist from falling forward in the sedge left specks of fern and sphagnum moss in his beard. Tears kept falling until he covered his head, bowed forward and howled with grief.

Colin had thought a week ago that everything in his world was going according to plan. He had just been promoted at the bank to assistant chief clerk, with a very nice pay rise, and he had upped his savings account with a belief that he could marry Lesley all the sooner. True, he had not asked her outright or got the ring yet but everyone knew they were going to be married, didn't they? Then there was the flat. It was easier to save while he lived with Mum and Dad. The house was big and they did not seem to mind what he did in it. He was the youngest of three; David was 28 and had finally married in Birmingham where he had worked as an accountant for five years. He had a really solid marriage. Hilary was a jolly, down to earth woman and said what she meant. She was from the black country; reliable, sensible. She would do what was right by David, she would not let him down. They would have children, get on in life, get a house on a mortgage. David had a Ford Granada and played squash and golf at the weekends.

Then there was Maggie his sister. She was 26 and was still courting, planning to get married next spring to Derek. He worked in a garage but he was already a partner and a whiz at hill climbing. He had all sorts of friends with old cars always going off on rallies. Colin had been with him a couple of times. It was great. Didn't Lesley enjoy herself that time? She could have friends like that if she married him. Now everyone in the town would know she had given him the push. She would be telling all her mates at the stocking factory. She could have given that up if they had married.

Now she was laughing at him with all the factory girls. Some of them had accounts at the bank. They would come in and snigger at him in the lunch hour.

Colin's head produced more situations where he could be ridiculed and humiliated than he could bear to think about. She had called him boring. "A boring prick" was how she had put it. Why had she been so angry? He had only ever been good to her, never got drunk or angry with her, never tried it on, never run out of money or forgotten her birthday. He had always seen himself as romantic. They had their own favourite record, their own special place, their little anniversaries, their first kiss, the first time they said "I love you" their first petting session. Well maybe that was it. Had she wanted him to go further? She never said she did. Anyway he had never done it with anyone and it seemed safer to wait till after the wedding. Lesley must have had desires he missed completely. Was that it?

Colin could not see himself as anything but a good catch. True, Lesley was three years younger than him. She probably felt they had some living still to do before settling down. But she had never gone to college or moved away. She seemed a home loving girl who wanted to get married in the Abbey in a white dress and peach satin bridesmaids. Now she was more interested in flower power and beads. One of her friends got married in brown and orange with a bead headband!

Colin had lived all his 23 years in the same country town, where he went to school, was in the scouts, the Abbey choir, went to Youth Club and Air Cadets. A town where everybody knew everyone else, everyone went to one school and worked nearby. If you were lucky you got a job in the town itself. It was only three streets meeting at a cross, its black and white jettied buildings nodding happily towards each other across the street, clustered like chicks around the great brown and pink bulk of the Abbey and its monastic Hall and cottages. Within a few hundred yards the three rivers that embraced the town on its long island hummock drew a line between civilization and the wide water meadows that spread as far as the eye could see, in summer grazed by black and white cows and Cotswold sheep. In spring the Welsh snows melted and turned the countryside into a waterland of lake and marsh that shimmered pale and grey under March skies. The waters drained away in spring and the land, now re-fertilised, pumped its life into corn and hay and barley reaching a crescendo of harvest in August, when grain stores heaved with the weight of wheat and the barges left day and night with the milled grain to the ports down river and the rest of the world.

Colin had never sought the adventure of travelling away. His best mate Brian, was always on about the river and how the first step out of the door was the start of the journey of a lifetime. Brian had hankered for the wide world and was always hanging over St Johns Bridge watching the barges going down the great silver sweep of water and out to sea. Brian was somewhere in India now. He had sent a few cards at the start from Goa, Delhi, the Taj Mahal but they had stopped about six months ago. Colin did not know what to do with them. He would have thrown them out but Lesley made him keep them. She had looked at them over and over, whereas he knew he would never go to India. So what was the point of keeping pictures of a place he would never visit? And how could he and Brian have drifted so far apart? Brian had hated Geography. He had had to copy Colin's work most weeks. They had both done maths together and Brian had said he wanted to be an accountant and now he had spoiled his career by going off round the world.

Then there was Martin. The three of them always went around together, shared a tent in Scouts, went on trips with

Air Cadets together, started their own skiffle group in the Youth Club. Who would have thought Martin would have been daft enough to buy a guitar and go to London hoping to be a pop star? So far he had been in a beat group called The Crowd and been a roadie for the Kinks on tour three years ago but seemed to have been on the dole and shared a two bed flat with three other guys. He had asked Colin to go down and visit and Colin had meant to but he was secretly worried they would smoke pot or take purple hearts and make him look stupid so he had used Lesley as an excuse. Maybe he should have taken her with him?

So now he was a man about town in the countryside, looked up to and respected by his parent's generation but largely ignored by anyone under twenty five. He was not averse to meeting George from the bank at the Hop Pole on Thursdays and belonged to the Lions. He liked doing voluntary work for people around the town and they all treated him with such gratitude and kindness. Then there was the annual round of events in the town, like the pageant in summer when he got his medieval knights costume out, resprayed the knitted chain mail with paint and marched through the town.

There was the Mop Fair in October when the town fell into wild abandon, funfair rides filled the streets and people from all walks of life crowded into the town for gambling, fighting and drinking and if the desire for abandonment and debauchery resided in the minds of the townspeople it was expressed in those three days unlike any other practice in the town for the other 362 days. Encouraged by the encroaching dark of winter and the last chance of celebration before the wet and cold drove people off the streets, as well as a habit of 800 years, the town cut itself off to traffic and filled the streets with machines of towering velocity, fixed within inches of the nodding gables of medieval houses. The uplit jetties and roofs aflame with garish light and unnatural noise took on a deep pagan significance. Colin could always feel the change in mood and functioning of the people of the town. Personalities altered, people drew out their hard earned cash and gave up their dour and diligent industriousness to rush from alehouse to alehouse, to dance among the stalls and carousels and try their hand at any silly game that would relieve them of their money. By Monday all returned to normal as if nothing had occurred and no mention made of the misbehaviour, the hangovers and the abandonment of morals. If by July a baby or two took on a look unlike its father, nought was said if a little Romany blood appeared here and there. It was a way of bringing new blood to a community that was self-sufficient for far too long.

Colin had little to do with the town's other traditions. His parents went to church on high days and holidays but God was never mentioned at their house so Colin grew up with an expectation of his all-seeing power without any benefit from his existence. For centuries many of the men of the town had had little discernable employment and worked according to the weather and the season. Elvering, reed cutting, salmon fishing, fruit gathering and harvesting had brought most of the income into the town before industrialisation and for many these still supplemented their dole money. Women did better, having the stocking factories, shop work and assembly work in the new industrial estates. Men had the mill, the farm work and electronic engineering for which warehouses were springing up everywhere.

Nor had Colin inhabited the summer meadows down by the Ham in the heat of summer. Nights when half the town seemed to be groaning with pleasure in dells and shadows beyond the bushes with anyone who did not happen to be their wife or girlfriend. He recognised something deep and irresistible was taking over the usually staid and devout members of the town as well as wayward lads and lasses at this time of the year. A tradition older than the Mop Fair or even the Church Calendar drew people down to the warm earth and the deep waters to regenerate the spirit and the seed of mankind. The power of this annual rite did not escape him but he never felt able to participate. He felt much as he did about going to Church. The events on the Ham were not talked about but probably drew the same proportion of townsfolk to it's strange rites as attended the church services.

Now all thoughts of parallel lives and alternative choices left him with a sense of emptiness where all his trophies and achievements shrivelled to nothing and he could recall no experience of which he felt proud or inspired enough to fight for Lesley's attention. He did not own a motorbike, or have a gang of drinking mates who exchanged quips and wisecracks. He did not smoke drugs or wear hippy clothes or know or care about protest marches or sit-ins. Nothing he could think of seemed exciting or adventurous and now he was being punished for his lethargy by losing Lesley.

It had not occurred to Colin that his smugness and his rigidity was in fact arrogance against his fellow men. He had spent his few years doggedly following the plan prescribed by his parents and their parents before them and in doing so he believed he was superior to his colleagues and acquaintance who were taking chances and making mistakes with their lives that fed and expanded their minds and imaginations. It was this arrogance that had driven Lesley away to seek a less stifling existence elsewhere and left him maimed and vulnerable. He had only loved Lesley and no one of his acquaintance had ever rejected him before and the shock was intense. He felt reviled; he felt repulsed by his body, he feared to look on his face because this was the body, the face that Lesley no longer loved. He wanted to smear his face with river mud and rend his clothes and run amok in the wild, but all he could do was slump towards the wet earth and sob.

On his back the late September sun tapped him on the shoulder as it raced from behind a puff of cloud. The earth and turf was strong in his nostrils and as he leaned over the green moistness he became acutely aware of the scent and sound of the marsh and it's wild birds and fauna. After a brief while he wiped his face with his shirt sleeve and looked ahead. He cared not if neighbours witnessed his grief.

"I saw your Colin down on the Ham, he was on his own; he looked like he was being sick".

He continued to whine and grizzle and as he gradually raised his gaze to the horizon it was few moments before he began to notice how different the river and the land appeared. The deep channelled river no longer existed but a broad sparkling silver bow lay ahead thick with duck and water birds and a quantity of shrubs and scrub grew in clumps all over the water meadows where there had been a hay field. No mill blotted out the skyline to the north, nor bridge nor sewage works and to the south the line of trees that followed the road was now a dense wood rising up where once the main road had run straight and unbroken.

His brain snapped into functioning and, still on his knees, he spun around to find the town, the Abbey Tower, the high Tudor chimneys and rows of beamed cottages were gone and replaced with a line of squat huts from which rose spirals of blue smoke and from whose environs could be heard the murmur of voices, a barking dog and the hammering of metal. Colin looked down at his clothes. He still wore blue jeans and his brown and beige Peruvian jumper, his blue and white check shirt and his hush puppies but the world around him had transformed into a wilderness. He stood up unsteadily, using his hands in the mud to push himself up and stood, alone, in an alien landscape.

Where St Mary's Lane had stood he saw a low line of round mud coloured dwellings with thatched roofs. The mill stream, no longer trammelled was a boggy marsh at the edge of the Ham. Before it stood tall black piles that formed a palisade against the water and where the mill restaurant had been was a rough jetty of hewn logs stretching out into the meadowland. Nearby grazed a herd of small brown sheep, like goats, with coarse hair and horns of a breed he had never seen before. Beyond, where once the Abbey had proudly dominated the town, the land rose surprisingly steeply but was crowned with dense trees. Oak and birch, yellow in the autumn sunshine.

The busy town to the north no longer existed and stark and clear he could see the high ridge of the hills beyond, forested except for the bare summit where there appeared to be some men pulling an ox. The earth on half the area appeared a rich sandy, red colour, new ploughed. To the south, also thick with trees, where the slate roofed council offices had been he could see a dark mass against the skyline but he could not make out what it represented.

Colin was struck dumb and immobile. In one second his world had disappeared. At first he gazed in awe at this mellow countryside but some few moments passed before he realised this meant he had no home to go to. No Mum or Dad, no Lesley, no London, no India. He began to stumble towards the huts, making for the jetty in the distance, his mind a tangle of confusion. How had he got here? Had he had amnesia and walked off somewhere else? But this was his home town, he recognised the skyline without the buildings without any doubt. The landmarks were still apparent, the sweep of the great river, the mound on which had stood the Abbey, the raised edge where the houses were built above the flood levels, he knew them well. He could not grasp the ideas in his head. Had he wished to die and was dead? Had he prayed and been answered in some way. Whatever the answer some great transformation had taken place as the result of his anguish and nothing would ever be the same again.

CHAPTER 2

THE VILLAGE

As he moved haltingly towards the huts he was startled by a movement to his left. From the bushes there suddenly appeared a wiry, brown skinned man, some six inches shorter than himself. Colin was no athlete but he realised this man was apprehensive about his greater size and was watching him suspiciously. Colin had time to judge his demeanour and gear and recognised what appeared to be a tribal person reminiscent of sketches he had seen of iron-age peoples. His hair was cut short and was thin and straggly. He was dark with deep set brown eyes and leathery weather beaten skin; thin lipped and lined. He reminded Colin of a picture he had seen of a bog body; an ancient man preserved in peat that had recently been discovered intact in Denmark. The man's clothing was surprisingly sophisticated. He was bare legged, but wore something knitted like short trousers below a tunic of coarse woven wool. The sides and shoulders were whiplashed with leather thongs and the open neckline laced similarly.

The blanket-come-tunic was the same colour as the sheep, a brownish beige, but the hem bore a band of yellow colour woven into it, and the whole held together with a metal buckle. On the belt hung a number of items. A knife, unsheathed, made of wood bound about an iron blade, not too good a condition but the blade edge looked recently sharpened. Colin guessed it could slit a man's throat if necessary. A pouch of soft leather also hung down and looked empty. Across the man's back a bow and quiver of arrows and in his hand two ducks. A hunter going home for his lunch.

The man glared back at Colin, ready to flee if necessary, but curious also. Once he realised Colin showed no aggression and appeared more fearful than himself he allowed his glance to stray towards the village, judging the distance from help if needed. This gave the man confidence and he spoke. No language that Colin recognised but if he had been told it was Welsh he would not have been surprised.

He tried to make sense of what the man might be trying to say. "Who are you?" no doubt, so he said "Colin" pointing at his chest. He repeated it and the man spoke some more but Colin felt unable to respond. What was the point in explaining when he did not know why he was there either. The man got a bit more aggressive when he witnessed Colin's evident vulnerability and motioned towards the village. Colin meekly walked ahead and although he could not think what action he could take it seemed reasonable to seek help with other humans.

They presented an odd spectacle if any had been there to see. The tall, thin, pale skinned man in modern dress slowly pacing towards an unknown destination and the swarthy little man behind chiding him along but moving fast to keep up with the pace. As they approached the jetty two small boys near the other end stood up and called to the other members of the village. From the nearer huts mostly women appeared, like his protagonist, wiry, dark skinned and dark haired. They all wore the woollen tunics girded round but Colin noticed that the villagers wore woollen cloth bound around their feet and tied to wooden pattens which raised them above the inevitable mud. The children ran almost naked, the older boys in rough loin cloths but the girls who appeared were clothed as the women. All appeared to be engaged in one task or another and put their work down to come and look at the stranger. Gradually twenty or so women and two older men gathered round him in the centre of the huts and stared. His captor was already bragging how he had tamed the tall man and brought him home. There was suspicion especially from the old men, who clearly had many questions to ask. The young women could barely resist examining his clothes, the rough knitted jersey they recognised but the cotton shirt and its fine stitching and cuff buttons was a miracle to them. One pulled at the fastening to see how it worked and the wiry man ordered her away. He handed the two ducks to a plumper woman, who stood placidly smiling at Colin, and gave her instructions and she took the fowl away. They disappeared in the direction of the blue smoke fire with their trophy looking back all the while.

One of the older men began haranguing the wiry fisherman and pointing south to the area where the council offices had once stood which Colin could now see was a log palisade surrounding some sort of building. An argument ensued. Colin felt if he suddenly upped and ran they would be taken by surprise and he could probably run faster, but for how long? When had he last run several hundred yards let alone a mile or two? These men were sinewy and muscled despite their small frames and anyway, where could he run to? He stood among them looking down helplessly as the black eyes and dark faces stared up at him fascinated.

Eventually the three men came to some sort of agreement and one marched off in the direction of the palisade, a mile or so away while the other pushed him towards the centre of the village. There were approximately fifteen to twenty round huts straggling around an area of baked mud. In some places reeds were strewn down, presumably against the mud, and there was an area of rough seating made from hewn logs and woven withies. The old man and the hunter had designated seats, the old man's stool with a rough canopy of sewn sheep skins held up by hazel stems had its back to the larger of the huts and formed a focal point of the village. He sat and then continued to pronounce; presumably about Colin.

The plump woman had taken the ducks, put sticks through them and they were baking over an open fire surrounded with stones. To one side a large clay oven sat on stones over a hearth where brands still smouldered and two of the girls were delving inside and pulling out what looked like large scones. There was a good smell of baking, sweetness and a tangy savoury scent coming from the large pot over the open fire. He hoped they would offer him some food as he was suddenly hungry, despite feeling that morning that he was too distressed to ever eat again and had had no breakfast.

The old man talked. Occasionally the others spoke too but the remainder listened. Here was hierarchy. The man prevailed and age was revered. Youngsters knew their place. More children had gathered and began fingering his clothes and shoes but were shooed away by the women. Not all were dark with brown eyes. Two of the younger women, obviously sisters, had black hair and deep blue eyes. Their skin was fairer and it's similarity to Colin's colouring was noticed. They giggled and flashed their eyes at him and reminded him of the factory girls with whom Lesley worked, interesting but unfathomable, dangerously unknowable.

The older man who had remained had greying hair but it was apparent he had had reddish hair and his beard still had traces of auburn in its depths. His tunic had a cloak of woven cloth and it was fastened by a large brooch of blood red coloured stone. They waited some time before the other village elder could be seen returning from the palisade. More "scones" had been made and placed inside the oven and these were now being pulled out by the girls and piled on a broad pottery platter. When the man returned he sat on a stool next to the older man and gave his speech of few words. The elder raised his hand and made a pronouncement. Colin began to feel a sense of desperation. Obviously people somewhere were starting to make decisions about him. He was not threatened in any way but these foreign speaking natives had taken over all decision making power and he could do nothing about it. No action ensued. One of the elders motioned him to join the others by sitting on a log near the circle of women. The cooked ducks were presented to the elders, filleted on platters of rough grained material. The bones were put in the pot to flavour a broth with vegetables and greens which the women poured into rough cast bowls and ate with a coarse bread. Colin noticed that even some of the younger women's teeth were worn down and soon discovered why. The "scones" of bread were full of grit from the millstone. He began to feel miserable, his hunger abated. Would he be living like this forever now? No Wimpy bars or pubs, no Mum's Sunday roast, no toilets? No hot baths or TV? A deep sense of loneliness overtook him and he fell silent and cowed.

His new acquaintance did not notice. The men talked among themselves seriously. The women threw curious glances at him and laughed. When they had finished the children were sent to the river to wash the crockery although they had licked and wiped the bowls clean already. Colin was aware there was no salt in the cooking so he did not feel thirsty like when he had soup at home. The men were drinking something from a large stone jug but did not offer him any and he had water like the children and drank from a ladle. The water was sweet, not river water and he wondered where they got it from. After the meal the women moved away from the hearth and in small groups sat outside the thatched huts weaving or knitting. Two girls were using a millstone under a canopy to grind raw grain which looked like oats.

He did not feel at liberty to walk around although no one seemed to want to stop him, but he noticed some buildings further down which were not housing. An area with reed screens appeared to have some sort of industry going on behind it, smoke in a thin blue stream rose up and he could see two boys furiously pressing alternate sets of bellows made from skins and sticks. Three little girls minded goats on tethers on the rough grass beyond.

Everyone seemed to have their job, however tiny they were. The oldest woman he had seen was not much past forty and apart from the three older men he had seen there were only teenage boys not old enough to have beards. He must have appeared very old to most of them and it gave him a queer feeling to be in a society where he was one of the older men. Where were the other men? As the afternoon wore on there sprang up a sharp breeze from across the river and there was discernable change in the mood of the camp. The women more frequently glanced up and looked towards the hills where Colin had seen the plough men. After a while, he saw, coming down a rutted track two oxen pulling a cart with three men walking beside it. On the cart were some large jars with lids. The men looked tired and plodded along unspeaking. They were greeted at the village with affection by one family of women who were quick to point out the stranger in their midst. Two were obviously brothers, dark and muscular, and about Colin's age, and came to look at him with suspicion. They deferred to the older men before inspecting his clothes. They were most interested in his shoes and wanted him to take them off but the leader spoke sharply for them to move away. Colin wished he could be like people in the movies where the hero produces a watch or a compass and mesmerises the natives but he had left his watch on the dresser that morning and had only a pen knife and some coins in his pockets as well as his door key, nothing that would startle them into submission.

After a short while, when they had prodded and explored him more than he cared for, he noticed the women clearing away their tasks and another group of men came up the track from the other direction. They carried spears, metal tipped, bows and quivers full of arrows. Between them on a stick were hares and ducks hung in pairs and behind two men with a small deer came smartly up the rear. A hunting party. Colin saw the girls rush forward to greet them and admire their catch and the three farmers looked sullenly after them. Clearly there was a hierarchy that revered hunters more than farmers. He wondered where the fishermen fitted in to the pecking order. The men washed in the river and went into various huts to dry off. The two brothers went together to the weaver women's huts, the third farmer to a hut alone and all four hunters went to huts with other women and children. Colin counted the buildings; eleven huts, two reed "sheds" and the animal compound. The little girls had put the two goats with the cow and were pushing green vegetation over the wattle fence. As it grew dark a group of small boys and two thin dogs rounded up the small brown sheep from the Ham, herded them expertly across a wooden bridge and put them in the compound as well. The two dogs lay down by the gate and were given bones to chew.

The women set about skinning the hares and plucking the ducks, throwing the offal to the dogs. They collected the feathers into skin pouches according to size and women took them away. The skins were washed and stretched over large stones and some paste spread over the insides. No one touched the deer that remained strung between the poles, now standing upright. The rabbits were cut up roughly and put in the large communal pot to stew with herbs and greens and some sort of whole grains. The ducks were wrapped in leaves tied up and put on hot stones round the fire to bake.

When it came to dinner time the men sat all together in the eating circle and had the pick of the duck and rabbits. The women sat further down, some bringing their work stools towards the fire, the children sitting around their feet. Colin was banished outside the circle at the insistence of the younger men, away from the women. They seemed to assume he would not wander away. Perhaps there was nowhere to wander to? He was given just the broth and the coarse bread again, like the women, but the women who belonged to the older men were offered some meat. After the plates were wiped clean with the bread two girls went to the oven and pulled out more scones which turned out to be honey cakes and one of the elders indicated he should be given one also. Colin began to realise there were subtle interactions between these people. There was a pecking order but rules could be broken. The women knew their place but were quite assertive in their manner. The elders wanted the stranger to know they could be magnanimous, to acknowledge they were aware of his superiority but not influenced by it. Their technology may be primitive but he had little difficulty understanding their mentality.

To his surprise, once they had finished the meal, the four hunters stood up and two came towards him and beckoned that he should follow. The other two collected the deer on a stick and the little party set off on the southern track. Colin felt cold but the other men were bare armed and bare legged still. In the dark he was aware of the silence all around him. The stars pricked out in an amethyst sky and nothing disturbed them. From the marshes, high pitched squeaks and the occasional click sounded clear and loud and a screech owl flew out from the trees. Behind them they left the flickering camp fires and up ahead the glow from behind the palisade was red. Colin realised he was going to meet the chief.

The path went round the base of a steep mound, grass covered. It was oval in shape and at one end the path cut up through the slope to a gate in the palisade where two guards stood with spears. They greeted the hunters and stared at Colin in the darkness. Once through the gate the torches in free standing sockets cast a hellish glow over the scene. Before him a high roofed hall stretched away fifty feet or more, smoke drifting from the centre to the roof. The walls of unhewn trees were bound together without windows. To one side another stockade held two or three horses and a barn ran alongside. A dog, tethered, bared its teeth at them and they went round the side to a tall door left ajar, with two armed men just inside who challenged them. One went inside and after several minutes indicated they should enter.

Colin was taken aback at what he saw. To start with he could hardly see for smoke which stung his eyes and caught in his throat. Apart from the central hearth there were small lamps like clay pots on a table beyond the fire. On each side were a dozen or so men sat on straw mattresses and beyond the hearth more men on wooden benches. Ahead was a table raised above the floor running across the end of the hall and a thick layer of reeds covered the floor between them, where lay a number of lean grey coloured hounds. Colin's eyes were streaming but he wiped his eyes and tried to see who occupied the top table. There were no women. In the centre a man sat, well made and strong featured. He looked about thirty five, dark haired and blue eyed with a broad forehead and square jaw. His clothes were significantly different, having a linen shirt below a leather tunic. On the shoulders dull metal clasps with a chased pattern singled him out as a wealthy man and on his wrist a torc that looked like gold, shone in the firelight. Before him stood a metal goblet. At his side sat three men. One, grey haired and bearded, held a knife with a bone handle as he finished his meal. On the other side two younger men, one dark haired but fair skinned like the chief, the other brown haired and dark skinned, looked up as the team of hunters filed in with their trophies.

Two of the men walked forward and presented the deer to the man who greeted them and waved them to the rear of the hall where a steward directed them through another door towards the barn. Colin was pushed forward and felt about as safe as the deer. The chief scrutinised him at length and ordered the men to pull apart his clothing. Colin meant to protest but three men nearby started forward with knives drawn. The Chieftan waved them a way but ordered Colin to take off his shoes. They were passed over to him for perusal and he looked closely at their making. He did not want to seem ignorant and handed them to one of his acolytes. Colin stood in his stockinged feet on the rushes with tears streaming down his face. The chief had no difficulty making him look ridiculous. He asked Colin to roll up his sleeves and flex his arms, then take off his belt. The belt was retained. Eventually a man was sent through a curtain behind the dais and came out with a woollen tunic. It was tossed towards Colin and it was made clear he should accept it as a barter for his own clothes.

The chief questioned Colin's minders and gave them some instructions then they turned him round and left the hall. He hobbled back to the camp, his socks in his pockets, but was grateful for the heavy wool tunic that kept out most of the damp and cold that now crept up from the river. The landscape was obscured by a thick mist as they made their way down the track. By the time they reached the village, people were gone inside their huts, the fire smouldered and crackled and the animals in the compound sighed and lowed together. Colin was drawn into a hut where the single man had disappeared and the two hunters followed him in. There were five pallets there with animal skins and the men lay down together in the darkness, talking all the while. Colin was grateful for the darkness as it afforded the only privacy he had had since his strange journey. He wrapped himself first in the wool tunic and then in a deerskin.

The smells assaulted him as strange and powerful, musk, sweat, earth, fur, wet wool, damp reeds. He quickly fell asleep exhausted and relieved to be leaving this dream for dreamland.

CHAPTER 3

THE SANCTUARY

Colin awoke the next morning and groaned when he realised the dream was not to end. He had slept reasonably well with no disturbance but now the other men were rousing themselves. They seemed to ignore him at first and dressed and scratched and yawned to themselves but as they were leaving signalled that he should get up too. Colin noticed that the hunters did not wear shoes but some of the older people wore pattens, bound to their feet with strips of leather. Now he had lost his hush puppies Colin decided his first task would be to beg or barter for a pair of these, for with a pair of these his feet would remain reasonably dry if not warm.

The weather was autumnal, mild but misty, and Colin guessed it was about five am as the sun was not yet rising in the east. The camp was stirring and women were re-kindling the hearth and oven fires with flint and tinder. Colin felt a sudden pang of nostalgia when he remembered learning about fire at scouts. He had started at cubs and had always been practical and won all his badges. He remembered writing a short essay on methods of lighting fires all round the world. He sat on the edge of the arena feeling disoriented and helpless and wondering what these people intended doing with him.

It was clear they lived in peace. There were no signs of defences against possible attack. Although they guarded their animals at night and kept dogs there was no sense of fear among the villagers. He marvelled how they functioned as a team. Everyone knew their job and went to it without demur. The young girls with leather sacks went across the Ham to the river to collect water, women mixed oats and meal in an earthenware pot and stoked the oven with wood brought by the smaller boys. The sanitary arrangements were functional. Towards the rear of the village was a large area for storing dung, rubbish and foliage and everyone used the dung heap as a latrine. Its combined temperature and weight organically broke down the contents into a reasonable tilth. Colin could see there was a pit of some sort and assumed they would dig it out and use it at some time of year. There were chickens and some hairy piglets rooting around for scraps and they ran, squealing, to and fro among the dogs and people. Colin supposed they would be fattened for the pot eventually.

There seemed to be plenty of food to eat although it was only recently it had been harvested. Over the Ham there were far more wildfowl than he had recalled, comprising of duck and geese species as well as swans and wading birds.

He had seen two hares hanging inside one dwelling and they also had their little brown sheep that were numerous. Once killed a pig or sheep would go a long way. Whether or not deer would be the province of the chief as in later centuries he did not know but guessed this was feudal tradition. In early Britain the game would have far exceeded what he was familiar with and the population less than a million. Feudal systems developed out of a scarcity of game when only the rich could take wild animals for food and pheasants poached on pain of death.

The grain was stored in the huts of the women, it appeared, and they ground it between great grindstones on the ground. Whether there was a variety or not he could not tell but he assumed it was oats. He later discovered they kept combs of honey in jars and mead in sealed jugs. They were proficient in making articles. Their pottery was thick and crude but functional and some of the pieces were quite large so they knew how to construct a big kiln and they had metal implements so they knew how to smelt. He had seen the chief wearing brooches to clasp his cloak of some intricate design with polished stones for decoration. They had rope and twine and he could see the huts were made with willow wattle from the marshes and reeds for the roofs. He could see the young girls engaged in weaving articles from reeds and willow and the young boys whittling branches in a concerted way that suggested they were making goods in bulk.

At breakfast time the villagers all gathered near the hearth, faced east and waited. The red sun broke the horizon and

29

they all raised an arm and murmured some incantation while the elder threw some libation on the ground. Breakfast consisted of the oat cakes eaten with hot milk from the sheep. Colin could taste some herby flavouring but not identify it. Caraway seeds? Aniseed? It tasted good and he began to feel grateful to these people who were so hospitable. What could they possibly think of him? No doubt if he had proved violent they would have tied him up and kept him as a prisoner but he felt by some sense of humanity that they would not kill a person unless they had to. They clearly had a belief system and social pattern that enabled them to live peaceably together. It was now about fifteen hours since he had arrived and for the first time he felt he should show some initiative in showing his thanks. He stood up, pointed at his bowl and held his hand up to the women, nodding and smiling. They grinned back. Body language was international and timeless.

As before, the children took the bowls to the stream to wash and the elders sat and gave instructions for the day. Two teenage youths were detailed to look after Colin but they did not seem to have any task to do. The two boys questioned him in their own language without response, examined his fly zip several times and laughed as they measured themselves against him. Colin had realised the night before he was at least 6" taller than anyone else in the camp. Most of the men were about 5'4" and he guessed the chief, who had remained seated, and his guards were not much more than 5'8". It gave him some sense of worth to be tall and have a belt and shoes to barter but he felt uneasy not having any plan or occupation to keep his mind sane. He realised that at some point he would need to learn their speech and felt depressed that he had never been good at languages at school. He decided he needed to put some structure into his strange new life.

First a calendar. It had been Saturday September 23rd when he disappeared from home so it must be Sunday 24th today. As long as he kept a record of the passing days he felt he could hold on to some sort of anchor in this madness. He thought if he could write down their speech he could at least recall phonetically words for things so he would need some means of writing and something to write on. It occurred to him then that if he ever got back home he could write a book about it and become famous. Lesley would soon come running then. They might ask him to tour the country giving lectures on how ancient people had lived here before. He had not listened much in history at school but he guessed these people were ancient Britons, pre-Roman. He wracked his brains to recall if anything Roman had been found in the town that he could identify if it was post roman or not but there appeared to be no buildings other than wattle and daub and the vista, of huts on stilts built over the river margins looked very like something he had seen in books on the Britons. They were sun worshippers too but he could only recall that all pre-Christians were the same.

Although he had been taken out of his own time it dawned on him that he was in the same place and the landscape at least was familiar to him. He recognised the long hump of Bredon Hill which rose up out of the vale of forests of oak and birch and the dinosaur shape of the Malvern Hills to the west. The river itself seemed quite different. Instead of running in a deep wide channel it spread out in wide rivulets and channels with islands between on which long reeds and tufts of willow grew. The spring floods he recalled from the other river would look just the same once the river level rose and filled all the flood plain below. He wanted to investigate where the town had been, where his house had stood, the Town Hall and the bank and the Abbey but he could see nothing but low trees and scrub all over the flat area between the Severn and Swilgate rivers. The track ran along the raised edge of the Ham where he recalled St Mary's Lane had curved and the Rose Garden by the Abbey Mill. There was just a raised area of oak wood where the Abbey would one day stand proud above the houses. Then he remembered the Tut. This was a rocky outcrop that stood high above the confluence of the Avon and Severn rivers and gave a view over the whole country side. He motioned to the two boys that they should set off in that direction. The boys called out to the elder, who was now ensconced in his chair by the fireside with a beaker of mead, who nodded in agreement that the stranger could go out of the village. They set off up the track going north through scrubby fields full of brown sheep grazing.

Colin pointed at one of their homes. "Hut" he said loudly. They laughed but did not get his drift. He persevered and pointed at a sheep saying its name as clearly as he could. After a half a dozen tries they started to get the gist and swapped names with him for everything from reeds to knives, and trees to toes. Colin picked up little of what they said but decided it was a start and possibly the boys would tell the others he was trying to learn. After half a mile they came to the confluence as the one great river swept into the path of the other and ahead, where in his time stood the St John's Bridge, he saw a long low wooden causeway built across the two rivers. As he drew nearer he realised the uprights were whole tree trunks driven deep into the river bed. He wondered how they could have achieved that. How old was this bridge? It looked aged with the posts encrusted with weed and green with rot but the bridge itself made of split timbers seemed quite new. They stood at one end staring at the endless span of water meadows. Colin wondered what was on the other side. More villages? A township and Roman town? He pointed at the bridge "Bridge" he said. "Punt" the boys shouted back. Colin stopped in his tracks. "Pont" was the French for bridge and in welsh as well. Were these the early Britons? He felt glad there might be some familiarity in the language but he could not recall any other welsh words he knew. He pointed to the outcrop of rock above them. "Tut" he said. "Tut" came the answer. For the first time Colin felt some grain of connection between himself and these people. The river had once separated two nations, Welsh and Danes. This town was right on the border and the tribes who lived right up to the river were eventually pushed right back into the mountainous regions by the Romans. He felt a surge of kinship. His Dad's mother had been Welsh, from Presteign, farmers for generations, and these people could be her ancestors after all.

He felt renewed with vigour and signalling to the boys, made for the Tut. The path came from the same direction, but where the concrete steps had been built in the 20th century here it was steeper and needed almost rock climbing skills to get up. Nevertheless when they got to the top and walked along the little path the summit was crowned with a wooden platform and on the North side a wattle fence had been erected. Signs of a fire nearby suggested this was a lookout for this tribe as it would always be until the end of the civil wars in the 17th century.

From the Tut he could see at least five miles across the river, as far as the Brecon beacons and north up the river valley towards Worcester. Nowhere could he see signs of buildings, camps or towns. The swathe of the river turned about one mile with its meandering streams and islets, cut through and endless forest north, south and west and only in one or two places could he see the telltale plume of blue smoke that indicated an encampment. One showed at the foot of the Malvern Hills and another somewhere beyond sight to the south. He wondered if Gloucester was there at all.

To the north the river sent up a great sparkling mist that shrouded out what lay beyond and the hills of Wales were obscured in the dazzling moist air of the valley. Despite his disappointment that he had probably hit on the only inhabited place for miles he saw the view as exhilarating and his memory of the familiar sights, the steel bridge, the waterworks, the farms and the far railway seemed artificial compared to this clean, untarnished spectacle of his home landscape. "Whatever happens to me I will never forget this experience" he thought to himself and realised sadly that in his heart his only hope was to be returned to his home as soon as possible by whatever means.

On their way down they saw two ponies with panniers laden with rock coming across the bridge. As they drew closer he could see it was a dull reddish rock and he wondered what they could be for. They descended the Tup, the boys still pointing and shouting out the names of every item around them, and rounded the bottom of the cliff. There in the lee was a clearing of quite industrial proportions. Three stone built edifices with burning ovens within were covered by a leather canopy. Beside were leather and wood pouches like great carpet bags on two sides of the building. To the north jutted out a wooden quay into the depths of the river and all around, piled up against the red rock of the outcrop, were great mounds of the same dull rocks.

As they walked towards the site the men engaged in shifting rocks and cutting wood with stone splitting axes stopped work and eyed them suspiciously, warding the boys away with words of warning. The boys whined but were rebuffed. However Colin could see that the three stone buildings that were about four feet high were furnaces of some kind. Kilns? Was this where they made the pots? Then it clicked the rocks which were piled everywhere was ore. This was a smelting works and he could see further along evidence of covered workshops and great stones used as work benches. This must be where they made their tools and armoury. No doubt they did not want their secrets known.

Colin had become interested in arms when they had studied the local battle at school. In medieval warfare a man was as good as his sword. Without modern methods of tempering all manner of secrets were handed down from one metal worker to another about how to make the hardest iron sword. It had since been discovered that most of the techniques of hardening metal had been known long before Roman times. Celtic metalwork was unsurpassed and while they were not a warring people they could defend themselves admirably. No wonder these men wanted no strangers discovering their secrets. He backed off with the age old hand signal of submission and they ignored him. However it made Colin realise how, in half a day, he had discovered several clues to the times he had fallen into. They had metal work skills, but no vehicles, they had communities but did not build in stone or mud brick, they had the rudiments of Welsh language and their distinctive belongings marked them out as Celts, iron-age Britons, living before the Roman Empire had ever been heard of. The people of stone-age circles, paganism and agriculture. Well worshippers and fertility invokers, who peopled Britain for 5000 years before the Romans came. He remembered all the Cotswold Hills were peppered with their tombs, stone circles and village sites and not twelve miles away one of the best excavated Neolithic sites existed on a hilltop overlooking the vale of the Severn. And here he was. Inside it with no one to tell.

Colin and the boys made their way back again. Colin was hungry and wondered what they ate for lunch. So far it had been pretty boring fare, gritty oat cakes and bread with watery soup. He thought the chief would be eating differently; tucking into roast venison probably. And what of home? Mum would be putting into the oven a joint of topside with a liberal dollop of dripping on the roast potatoes, parsnips and in the top oven a big apple pie and on top a saucepan of custard. There would be uncle Mac and the Goons on the radio and later the Clitheroe Kid. Dad would be down the Legion with a pint and his sister Maggie reading the News of the World, reading out the scandals to Mum in the kitchen. The Abbey bells would be ringing out when the service ended at 11.15 and they would all sit down together at 1 o'clock sharp to the best food he had ever tasted. Here there was no Sunday holiday. Day after day the same round of chores, and activities, cooking, weaving, harvesting, slaughtering, manufacturing, smelting and farming, round and round and round without interruption he supposed.

Colin spent his first week just like that. The success with "pont" and "tup" went round the village and the children gathered round him to try out all their other words. Colin could think of no other Welsh words except "eglwys" which meant church, and had no meaning for them, and Aber which meant river mouth and they looked blankly back at him. But every day was not the same. They all seemed happy to let him experience various aspects of their lives; the second day a girl of about twelve with a round face and deep brown eyes took him to the looms and showed him how they wove the spun yarns into cloth. All their wool was white and brown and was woven in stripes or with a brown and beige border. Looms in other homes had coloured wools in them, green and blue and yellow and the girl showed him the spun hanks of yarn hanging up in their roofs. He supposed the colours came from plant dyes or the earth but he saw no evidence of dying processes anywhere. There were ready made pieces of cloth folded and finished in one house as if ready for transport elsewhere and he assumed they exchanged cloth for some other commodity. But if they were self- sufficient what did they trade the cloth for?

On the fourth day the leathery man who originally found him beckoned him to join him and taking twine and hooks they headed back to the river edge to fish. The brown man who called himself something like Yarren knelt on the bank careful not to cast a shadow and putting a grub on the hook dropped it below the bank and let it dangle. Now fishing was something Colin was good at having been brought up in a region full of rivers, ponds and weirs and he knew exactly what Yarren was after, the big pike that was lurking in the peaty undercurrent of the bank. The willows leaned way over the water just as they did in Colin's day and he felt a pang of regret that he had not been carrying his rod and line when he disappeared from the real world. He would normally be ensconced half way along the bank between the weir and the lode with his brilliant tackle to fish with. It had taken him four years to save up for and bend to his will the bamboo rods and fast reel that he used for coarse fishing, not to mention his fly rod and his father's excellent flies. But the principle was the same and the river would no doubt have the same fish including salmon in season. He began to plan how he could fashion a willow rod and make some flies up out of duck down and some of their coloured wools if they would lend him some of their hooks. He had a knife at least.

He helped Yarren by seeking out the currents where perch hang motionless upstream and the deep pools where carp lurk and they had a successful day's fishing, returning with eight fat fish for the village and a variety of small fry. As before the men had the meat and the women and children the broth from the skin and bones and the dogs and pigs had any leftovers. But this time Colin got some fish. It was only half a fillet of carp but the men's eyes told him he was accepted as someone useful. Maybe that was the way forward? Show them a skill and they would accept him. For the next week or so Colin spent his time finding a suitable willow wand for a rod and fashioned some sort of winding mechanism out of wood. He whittled out a little reel but was unable to fit it effectively to the rod. The line was even more complicated. All artifacts were prized. Yarren's twine was his and his alone, his tool of work so to speak. Colin began to realise if you want something in this world you made your own. Fortunately Yarren guessed his need and showed him the source of his own line. To Colin's horror, in an earthenware crock near the dung heap were the collected intestines of the hares they had eaten, soaking in urine. The smell took his breath away but Yarren cheerfully plunged in his hand and pulled out several yards of gut and proceeded to show him how to shred it with his knife into finer and finer strips. The urine had suppled it so it remained elastic and Colin realised with clever knotting he could get as long a line as he required from one gut. Within two weeks he had a serviceable rod and line and twelve hooks courtesy of a youth who seemed to have connections with the smelters, and twelve fine flies.

Without the weir Colin had no idea where salmon would be most likely to be caught. He suspected beyond the smelters where the waters shallowed before the confluence but decided to try downriver of the bridge to start with. It was two days before he was successful but the hours of standing thigh deep in river water paid off and when he finally returned to the village with a fine salmon he reckoned at 12 or 14 pounds. Everyone ate fish that night. It was wrapped in some large leafed weed, baked in the fire and when the skin came off with the leaves it was all put in the pot for broth. Colin thought he had found his role in the village.

He had noticed the difference between how he was treated here and if something similar had happened in his day. The natives were cautious but not suspicious. They did not fear him but almost seemed to want to keep him with their village like a trophy. Maybe his height and size made him a desirable asset? They seemed to have no concept of a spy or treacherous behaviour and let him share their lifestyle straight away. True they had got the permission of the chief but what else could they have done? They could have killed him or locked him up but seemed to expect him to want to stay. Perhaps human life was truly valued here. Every strong man meant the survival of the tribe. Did this mean there was little to run away to? Would he have starved if he had gone into the hills? If he had joined some other tribe would they see him as a potential enemy? They seemed generally relaxed and pleased when he showed some usefulness.

A month or so after he arrived he was trying to perfect some of his flies when he noticed a stirring among the people late in the afternoon and into the village came the weirdest person. He was tall, taller even than Colin, and walked with an air of superiority and elegance. He was dressed in a white woollen gown that flowed around him as he walked and was edged in deep blue and at his neck he wore a brooch of gold and amethyst with snaked heads coiled around a face. His hair was long behind, bar from the forehead where it was shaved right back to the crown from ear to ear. His beard was tawny red and flowed down his chest in two long points. His nails were long like claws suggesting he did no manual work and on his feet he wore leather boots unlike anything the village people had.

He was greeted with great reverence and mothers pushed their children forward to receive his blessing. With him hurried a youth of great beauty; olive skinned and dark; clean shaven, he looked like a young Apollo, with his knee length white smock and bare legs and carried a large flat leather bag in his arms with great care. Behind them followed an old man with a grey pony laden with all manner of possessions. The man, or wizard as Colin thought of him, went straight to a hut where one of the women had been sick for some time. The old attendant undid parcels and bags and called for hot water and soon a water bowl with herbs infusing was taken into the sick woman. After half an hour the wizard took his leave and left for the wooden hall but not before he stopped to inspect Colin. Clearly he had been told of the appearance of this mysterious stranger but after holding Colin's gaze for several moments he left without another word. His attendant remained at the camp, leaving the youth to carry the leather bag and some parcels up to the hall. No doubt the wizard dined with the chief tonight.

The attendant was obviously known and very welcome in the camp. At night he slept in the hut of the elder and was given preferential treatment at dinner. He and the elders polished off a crock of mead and there was much laughter and singing after the meal. The days were still warm and nights, though chill, did not have the essence of autumn yet and Colin could sleep reasonably well with his sheepskin and socks on. At breakfast the sick woman came to join them for the first time in days. Colin noted that each day the ritual of welcoming the sun continued without fail. Of course he knew that each day it was 2 or 3 minutes later and he became quite attached to the ceremony shouting his greeting and thanks for getting through the night. In his world everything had become very uncertain and this was one thing he could bank on.

When he arrived at the village it had been a new moon and now a month or so later it was waxing again. At the full moon some of the men had gone out late and many of the women had stayed out after bed time. Colin took little notice of this change in routine and having walked miles along the banks to acquaint himself with all the pools and shallows and rock ridges in the river he was tired and went to his bed shortly after sundown. However three days after the wizard arrived he came to dinner at the village and one of the sheep was killed and roasted in his honour. Colin soon discovered the contents of the leather bag and why the youth handled it so lovingly; it was a beautiful golden harp or possibly a lyre, which Colin had only heard about. Colin was not musical and after eating there was a brief ceremony towards the moon and then he played. Colin was at once struck by the atmosphere he created and began to understand the meaning of the word mystical. He sat mesmerised by the fluid sounds of the boy's voice and the lyre while watching the clouds skim across the quarter moon and the whole of human history flew through his mind. Thousands of years before the ancient Greeks had sat like this beneath a foreign sky and felt the same thing, the power of the earth and planets, the fragility of man and the wonder of human existence.

The wizard, or bard, as Colin now recognised him, had thrown some herbs on the fire which issued a pungent scent and heady aroma and the mead bowl was passed between the men. His song was long and dolorous and Colin knew nothing of the words but felt the spirit of the music as a story of death and tragedy, war and pestilence followed by a triumph of clashing swords and survival. Perhaps it was Beowulf or a Mediterranean tale brought by the dusky youth. The villagers listened rapt for what seemed like hours.

Colin began to feel anxious that he would fall asleep and had a desperate urge to go to bed but guessed rightly that this would be an insult to their guest. Eventually he came to the end of the tale and the listeners let out cheers of appreciation and the elder made a speech of thanks. Colin was so grateful to be able to go to sleep he felt the second surge of joy on climbing under his sheepskin since catching the salmon. The next morning he would have slept way past dawn if the others had not woken him for the sun ceremony. However he felt inspired next day to improve his fishing skills and helping himself to another hares gut from the urine pot he made a long line to lay across water with several hooks to catch eels.

In fact now he was not preoccupied with problems at the bank and getting to football on Saturdays and worrying that Lesley was seeing someone else he felt quite inventive. He had made himself some serviceable pattens with leather straps that did not cut into his instep. He had got some yarn scraps and made himself a hanging calendar by placing bits of pierced bark, one for each day. He had used brown for September and now white for October and got the bark from where the boys did their whittling on what he now realised were arrow shafts.

Over the last weeks he noticed he had caught the eye of a sturdy dark girl of about fifteen who seemed keen to wash his shirt, socks and underpants and looked at him from under her lashes. At last he began to feel he was part of the community now he had a trade to offer and his periods of anxiety about getting home became less frequent.

As the moon waxed to the full the villagers became clearly restless and spent more time discussing and gazing at the familiar face of the moon. Finally the full moon arrived and an air of excitement pervaded the whole village by darkness. All but the youngest children and oldest women gathered after dinner, wrapping themselves close in wool blankets and shawls. They huddled together in groups chattering and nervously laughing until, at the call of the elder, they formed into an informal procession and slowly made their way towards the woods, chanting a solemn tune. Colin brought up the rear, at the last moments grabbing a wool blanket and his pattens. They walked first up the track and then in single file took a path to the left leading into the oak grove where one day the great 11th Century Abbey would stand. Beyond view in the trees was a clearing only 30' long but moss covered and within the trees were rough hewn standing stones, nine in a circle and in the middle one single monolith 7' or more clear of the ground. Already in the circle was the bard and his assistants; the chief and his men stood at one of the elliptical ends where another path joined from the hall and the villagers progressed round to the other end, standing among the trees where they could stand, or sit, children clasped to their sides. Colin realised immediately he was about to witness some pagan ceremony and it flashed through his mind he might have been the chosen sacrifice except no one took any notice of him. Then he remembered his bark and string calendar. That morning he had fed the last white bark piece for October. Today was Halloween eve, Samhain in the old calendar. What this meant was unknown to him other than witches and pumpkin lamps. In truth it was the day before winter started when the souls of the ancestors are remembered and communicated with but only with those versed in knowledge. This night the villagers had acquired a medium for their past and he would reveal any messages from the ancestors that was worth having or might warn or protect them in the future from evil or man-made misfortunes.

The bard looked ferocious in the light of a wood fire at the far end of the ellipse, his eyes were rolling in his head and instead of the golden harp his assistant pounded a skin drum in an incessant rhythm. In due course he circled the fire and began chanting and screaming out and working himself into a frenzied trance. Colin had seen a film about the Shaman once who did similar actions in order to contact the otherworld and he recalled it took some time to achieve.

At some point the old attendant brought in a young sheep that came so placidly Colin assumed it had been drugged. Before the monolith was a pit over which a large metal salver was laid and leading the lamb forward the Bard offered up incantations and produced a long bladed knife. At this point the villagers began to look up behind them for the position of the moon and the thick clouds scudding through the night on westerly breezes only allowed tantalizing glimpses. When the time was right the Bard, in one fell swoop, cut through the lamb's neck almost to the bone and there was a brief second before the creature capitulated; when one moment it was animal and then the next it was carcass and it fell forward guided so that the blood from its jugular gushed into the platter. Quickly the animal was taken away and gutted while the Bard thrashed and proclaimed around the monolith. Little gasps escaped the crowd as presumably he uttered predictions or messages from the ancestors. Colin tried to guess from the crowd's response whether the news was good or bad. Eventually the entrails were brought before the chief and the Bard, moving to the southern end of the circle, made pronouncements to the chief alone. He stood resolute and made no response but Colin felt the atmosphere tense.

Now the pronouncements were over the Bard was exhausted and led to a seat outside the circle to recover. The sheep and its remains were put into the pit and a blessing said by the old attendant. Colin was struck by the fact they did not use the meat for eating but supposed the "moon god" was supposed to have it. The crowd left promptly and having exited the wood, talked excitedly all the way home-good news presumably.

CHAPTER 4

BOAR HUNT

Colin's calendar grew. He now had three strings full and four pieces of bark on the fourth. 4th December. It made him think of Christmas, of not getting up early for four or five days and waking up to see frost patterns on the glass before Mum came in with a cup of tea. Auntie Vi arriving from Birmingham on Christmas Eve with her Yorkshire terrier in a basket and the Christmas pudding in her suitcase amongst the corsets and bed socks. Christmas was the time he felt most nostalgic and wanted to be at home with all the familiar things of home and he was 2000 years and a cosmos away in language and ideas. There had been some bright moments; he had learned a few phrases and two older teenagers seemed to have chosen him as their role model. They seemed to have heard about the chief and Colin's Hush Puppies and believed he had some magic abilities. Colin wished only that was true. The weather had got colder but nowhere near the biting frosts that he was used to, more like mid-November, moist and temperate, but his feet seemed permanently cold. He had given up wearing socks with his pattens as they got wet anyway and saved them for just in bed and it gave him a sense of security to be able to fall asleep with warm feet.

As the days shortened the villagers spent more time in their huts. They slept until just before dawn as usual and greeted their God as he came over the eastern horizon. His fellow hut sharers were three young men whom he called hunters and seemed restless and busy: they practiced spear throwing and had twine nets with stones at the corners for catching prey. Their main weapons were bows and arrows which they fashioned themselves with the help of one of the elders who appeared to be master woodsman. He was fascinated at how intricate their craftsmanship was. Their bows were small but each was made from three separate strips of wood from different trees bound together with leather and slowly bent into a distinctive shape which was springy but strong and most of the younger boys could easily fell a duck or hare at first try and were often successful with bigger fish too. They teased Colin into practicing with them but his co-ordination was so poor and the small bows so inadequate for his height he could barely fire an arrow and certainly not hit anything intentionally. Several times the hunters took him across the Ham, upriver or into the forests to hunt for small game but used him more as a gun dog than a performer. He beat out the wildfowl for them to fire at and waded thigh deep to retrieve injured birds and hares and on one occasion caught something that looked like a small turkey. He was the one who carried back the spoils hooked on a pole.

Colin had arrived apprehensive of what the villagers might do if he tried to leave. He had never done so and only saw the nearer forests and cultivated land with the hunters. He still wondered what lay afar. Were there other villages nearby? Presumably people settled where there was a natural feature or resources, like iron ore or a harbour or a ford. Tewkesbury had been a ford for as long as could be recalled. He knew that when the Danes and the Saxons debated a peace treaty they chose Deerhurst about four miles down river from there but that was eight hundred years later. Tewkesbury had always been the first crossing place of the Severn until the Romans built the bridge at Gloucester and the great Severn Bridge in the last decade. Colin tried to imagine a map of England in his head and remember where the towns and villages were and why they were there. Places in the Cotswolds like the Chippings and Stow were built in the medieval period from the wealth of wool and before that the Vikings and other Europeans had been invaders for several hundred years after the Romans left. Everyone had retreated to Hill forts to avoid capture and pillage. When the Romans had come they built strategic towns to occupy and colonise the locality; Gloucester, Cirencester and Bath were all big cities around 200 AD. All on rivers, all with access to cultivated lands with good soils. He searched his mind for any knowledge of the Romans in Tewkesbury but he had never heard of any. He wondered if they would let him go walking. He thought if he could get to Gloucester he might see something he would recognise; it was only ten miles south.

He decided to speak to the elder the next day. After the sun ceremony he approached him and made a praying gesture that served to say he wanted something. The elder was very decrepit and he was not so sure he could understand. He sat in his chair padded out with skins and his canopy much of the day and had taken to drinking hot posset now it was getting colder. In a patch of soil Colin drew the Severn, the village and the chief's camp. He drew the road south, pointed to his chest and did the finger walking action. The elder shook his head and looked at him hard. He called in two other men who looked at the picture and seemed to understand he wanted to go somewhere by foot. They deliberated and questioned him but Colin could not guess what they wanted to know. At last the three men shrugged as if to say "do what you want". Colin went and got his wool tunic, his pattens, his sheepskin and asked for some food from the women. He was given some oat cakes, dried pork and some nuts as well as some of the rough cider.

He did not know where he was going or for how long but he needed to know what was beyond the margins of his sight. As the sun was half up he set off on the path past the chief's camp. He wondered if the guards would stop him and as he rounded the base of the mound they stared suspiciously but made no move. He supposed that as they assumed he had come from another tribe he would want to return at some point and there was no reason to stop him. As long as he pulled his weight in the camp he was welcome to stay; maybe all newcomers were treated the same.

The pattens were not good for walking. After about half a mile he decided to walk barefoot and wondered if he could get to Gloucester without shoes. He should have asked for a pony. The track was quite clear though not as well trodden as it had once been.' He could see the margins where it had once been but there were brambles and grass now and the path was lumpy and more intermittent. Fewer people walked here than had done so in the last decade. He saw lots of wildfowl on his route. There seemed an endless supply of ducks, geese and swans and other small water birds ducking in and out of the reeds and marshes. Like the A38 the path ran away from the Severn keeping to a high ridge of land. He knew all the villages hereabouts, Appleby, Norton, Staverton, but there was no sign of life now, not even a plume of smoke. He walked for an hour to where Coombe hill was a high spot in the landscape. But had seen nothing but forest, marsh and scrub and he began to feel rather lonely. He was five miles from the village but there was no sign of any other settlement. He began to develop fears of what might be beyond. Perhaps the village was unique. Maybe he would get to Gloucester and be captured or enslaved. If there was a harbour there he might get press ganged on to a ship. He hated sailing and knew nothing about oars and ropes and seamanship. He sat on a fallen tree in a copse of hawthorn and decided it must be lunchtime. He took out his oat cakes and pork and then realised he was nowhere near water to get a drink. He searched his memory but could not think of any tributaries to the Severn on this side. He thought of the characters he had come to know in the village, Mard and Arna and Morga and Yarren and the dark haired girl who looked after him every day. He began to feel that they were the nearest thing he had to family now. While in his mind he was walking to Gloucester for the day in reality he could be walking to his death; warring tribes, pirates, Roman soldiers, he had no idea who could be waiting for him in five miles time. Even worse there might be nobody there at all, just an ever spreading estuary of the Severn flowing out to sea and miles of mud flats.

He sat and tried to make up his mind. He looked west to where the Malverns seemed even closer, their teeth-like profile even more familiar to him than anything he saw now. He remembered family expeditions over the crest when you could stagger up the steep side and then triumphantly sit on the summit surveying Wales and England to the horizon. What would he see from there now? Would any of Wales be populated? Surely people dwelled where there were animals in the forest or valleys to be cultivated. When he thought of the hostile uplands of the Brecons and the Black Mountains he wondered could people exist there now?

He sat for a long while feeling gloomier and more anxious by the minute. At least in the village people were kind to him; he was popular. The dark haired girl was always smiling at him. He would never starve even if his hut was spartan and his fare was the most basic of all the villagers. He just could not see where it was all going. Logically he should be a soldier- he was bigger and much more solid that the others- but his attempts at bowmanship were pathetic. He could never kill anyone with a sword or knife. The sun started to set in the west and he decided the last thing he wanted was to be trapped out here in the world after dark. Suddenly his straw pallet and sheepskins appealed more than anything to him and he stood up, saluted the sun and set off at a brisk pace homewards.

By the time he reached the chief's hall it was getting dark and his eyes were more accustomed to the dusk. He was sure he could see a lot further than when he worked at the bank and he could see the outline of the palisade against the northern skyline quite clearly from about a mile away. In the bushes he could hear the sound of birds and larger animals scurrying away and wondered if he could survive a night out under the stars. The guards drew their swords as he approached and he stopped and raised his hand in submission. They were two different men from those he had passed in the morning so it took one to recognise him and tell the other to sheath his weapon. When they motioned him to pass he gave a jaunty salute.

Soon he saw the smoke and red glow of the village fires, heard the bark of a dog and the squeal of children playing. Never had he been so relieved to be back in such a strange place before. He walked into camp startling a few people at first then those around the fire turned and greeted him. His two young acolytes came up, presumably asking where he had been. He felt embarrassed that he was empty handed in case they thought he had gone hunting. A visitor had arrived before him, selling something from a pony with a small boy servant. He was telling tales and played a small pipe between stories. It was an eerie sound over the crackling twigs of the fire and lowing of the animals. Out here in the empty darkness of the landscape these people had made a world that was warm and welcoming and an oasis in a wilderness of cold and hostility. Colin was invited to join them. Hare soup and millstone grit bread had never tasted so good.

The next day he awoke in his sheepskin cover, his warm socks on his feet and his head on a goose feather pillow and thanked God he had not walked away. He had to learn to live in the world as it was not civilized England in 1970. He began to realise that he had hoped that if he walked far enough he could get back to the future. That somewhere on the road to Gloucester he would wake up and be home again; but he had to get that idea out of his head for good. Life was here and now: people were kind and fed him and put a roof over his head. What they had to do to enable him to live in this hostile, wintry place was quite heroic he now knew.

Having come back without food he felt humble. No one had deprived him and he could not say he got less than the average worker but he was aware the elders were fed first and they had been hunters. His own three room mates were always out and about, taking their spoils to the chief and he assumed they got fed there along with the soldiers. Catching deer and other wild animals was worth a reward and although they did not need motivating it was in everyone's interest to keep them happy.

He had had time to think about their prey and recall some of his history. There were chickens, but they did not seem to eat them. Their horses were no more than small ponies ridden without saddles and they did not kill their cattle to eat at all. Deer were everywhere but rarely killed and he assumed it was the prerogative of the chief's men to hunt them. There were no cats or grey squirrels, no magpies or doves, no pheasants anywhere to be seen. He had seen small animals in the forest; long red coloured creatures inhabited the trees as well as red squirrels and he had seen stripey piglets running through the undergrowth. There was an abundance of game to be eaten but they had to be caught and it was on a brisk winter morning that Colin became aware that the men from the chief's hall were in the village gathering together a hunting party. One of the older men sought him out and directed him to join the party. Colin had previously gone on expeditions in the pattens and wool rags but they were not easy to run in and he noticed the other youths were strapping on leather gaiters to protect their legs in the undergrowth. He pestered his room mates until one of them found him a pair to strap on and and he was provided with a spear with an iron tip wedged and bound into the wooden shaft of ash strengthened with leather bindings. It had clearly seen better days, the white ash of the shaft being stained with old blood. Colin followed the group of about fifteen men past the smelters and north down the main track. After a mile they turned off into the forest led by a village man who appeared to be a tracker and several men from the hall. His room mates followed up the rear with the twine nets and ropes.

Colin began to feel uncomfortable; shooting for ducks and hares was acceptable when you were hungry but why this large party and the extra spears that were carried in bundles? He started wondering about woolly mammoths and cave bears but his worst fears did not prepare him for the day's activities. After about an hour, when the sun came up out of a watery green sky and filtered through the now defoliated boughs the tracker became more and more animated, sniffing and rubbing spoor and inspecting tracks in the leaf mould. The group of men stopped where the increasingly thick undergrowth led towards an incline to the west and Breedon Hill, as he knew it. rose behind stark and bare above them. The younger men began to unfurl the nets and pulled one out in full that was gradually tied here and there to stout young birches forming a trap between some bushes. Clearly this was the track of their prey. Colin tried to see the size of the spoor to assess what they were hunting but it did not appear large. Although he knew little about animal droppings it was not the size of an elephant. They worked in silence, hand signalling to each other and gradually spreading out in an arc on either side of the net. Colin was taken with one of his room mates and given two spears to hold. He could see their breathing was fast and they were tense with excitement, they peered and listened for any sign of movement in the thicket. Gradually on either side they worked their way back towards the hills, silently moving on leaf mould and holding their tongues.

Soon a slight snuffling and grunting could be heard and footfalls surprisingly loud on the crisp soil. The men seemed to know what to do instinctively, two or three staying in front of the prey while the others suddenly leapt behind clashing their spears and screaming. Out of a tangle of briars stormed a huge boar, bristling and foaming at the mouth. To Colin it seemed reasonably short in stature but the fury in its little mean eyes and the roaring in its throat when it saw the men beyond was terrifying. Somehow its gaze fell on Colin and as it leapt forward he felt his insides turn to water and legged it back down the path. It appeared enraged and foam flew from its jaws as it darted and charged from side to side, slashing with its tusks and trying to gouge each person. Men rushed from every angle and some ran forward and stabbed at the creature with spears, one catching the boar on its flanks and dragged behind so that it uttered squeals of rage. It tried to escape down its usual path and the men held back momentarily while it fled towards their net. More protagonists, including the now recovered Colin, closed in towards the kill. Colin assumed that once caught and netted the animal would be easy to dispatch but it tore relentlessly at the twine and its energy and force were so intense it drove its way clean through, dragging the net behind, stones and all. At this point the entire crew approached and with all their amassed strength forced their spears into the head and neck. Colin was appalled but felt obliged to stab again with his spear but closed his eyes as he did so and the solid flesh and hide resisting his thrust like a small prick. The hot blood pouring out was shocking and the smell of fear and gore made him feel dizzy.

Two stronger men had rushed from the front and were spearing the animal in the jaws, but not until both had flung their entire weight on to the spears and stood their ground did the animal show any sign of resignation and boiling bloody froth spouted from its nostrils and mouth. Again and again the youths thrust; one got his spear up and into the boars ribs piercing the heart and with a gallant snarl it fell to its haunches, collapsed and fell silent.

Colin could not remove from his memory that little beady eye which rolled in his direction full of recrimination and a pang of guilt ran through him. If ever there was a moment to become vegetarian this had to be it. He recognised that for centuries people had bought meat from a seller without having to face the hideous reality of slaughter and that every meat eater in the country save slaughtermen were absolved of the horror of murder. Colin was not regretful he had failed to impress with his hunting skills despite his greater weight and height. The chiefs men pointed at him and laughed at his fears and the village men looked away in embarassment but Colin thought at least he would not be expected to go on any other hunting expedition again.

The men were elated and jumped and hugged each other like football players. Three men hung on to their spears to ensure the beast stayed down. The dark purple blood ran into the soil steaming and coagulating and the stench of gore turned Colin's stomach. It lay on its side, its eyes quickly glazing over and death was apparent. The men untangled the nets and used twine ropes to secure its front and back legs to two stout poles. This time it was not Colin's job to carry the spoils as no one else matched his height and it took six men to carry the weight on their shoulders. Colin's sleeve was plucked and it was indicated he should return to the thicket. He felt a sense of nervousness; surely they would not be after another one today? But he soon found the bushes alive with squealing piglets that the men were stabbing at for sport and urged him to join in. Colin threw his spear but was glad he missed as he was beginning to feel nauseated by their excitement. By the time he retrieved it the remainder of the piglets had run shrieking into the bushes and they had claimed another four beasts for the pot. Similarly parcelled on poles Colin did his share of carrying one piglet on a pole with the tallest of the hall men. The others laughed and jested with each other re-enacting the chase and kill and Colin thought how similar their mannerisms were to his friends after a football match; elated, merry and over stimulated. They crashed about in the woods feinting stabs at bushes and logs and yelping in mimicry of the dead boar. At the junction with the path to the hall the great boar was carried off for the chief's feast and the smaller piglets went with them to the village. By now it was early afternoon and they had not eaten for several hours. They were feted on their return and the children all ran and stared into the faces of the piglets with glee. Clearly roast boar was not on the menu that often and Colin felt there was a system whereby only the chief could decide when and how a boar was to be killed. The women greeted them with food from the day meal, duck stew and unleavened bread, and took away the piglets to be disembowelled. It was during that afternoon when the hunters lay on their beds recuperating that Colin got to thinking about the food he missed and what could be remedied.

Most of his favourite foods had yet to be invented-chocolate, roast potatoes and baked beans were still a continent away and apple pie and custard and Yorkshire puddings 1500 years into the future. He drooled at the memory of sausage and mash with gravy, liver and bacon casserole, beef stew and dumplings and fried chicken and chips. There was no corn oil for frying, no wheat flour for pastry or potatoes.

He searched his mind for memories of watching his mother cooking and what was required. Here they had flour for oat cakes and flat breads that did not use yeast and they had chicken and duck eggs, although he had not seen them using them in cooking. There was pig and mutton fat and intestines for sausages and with milk from the little brown sheep he began to set up a plan to be the first person to make toad in the hole.

The piglets were not cooked that day nor the next nor the next. He discovered they were being hung in one of the women's huts having the blood drained out of them and the entrails removed. Colin wondered how he could get them to change the habits of a millenium and figured he would need some kitchen utensils. When they roasted meat over the fire they let the fat drip into the ashes instead of collecting it for dripping. They used a spit system, one of the children being delegated to turn it now and then. In the clay oven they stewed the meat in the juices and mopped it up with the oat bread. Colin needed a metal tray to catch the meat fat and a jug to store the dripping in.

After two days he had persuaded the smelters to beat out an old bronze shield well past it's sell-by date into a flat dish with sides and on the 7th day which would have been the 11th December, persuaded the cooks to let him put the tray beneath the first piglet to be spit-roasted. Clearly this interfered with the usual method and kept the fire from under the middle but with some curiosity they allowed him to collect a quantity of pork fat. Colin watched the drips gathering to form a pool, then a reservoir until it was full enough to tip into an earthenware bowl. He did it about four times during the cooking of the piglet which took about 4-5 hours and the fat dripped faster and faster the hotter it became. He then had to persuade the cooks to let him have the intestines and some offal from the inside of the piglet, liver and heart, together with some of the belly pork from one of the hanging piglets. What was missing was flavouring and seasoning. They kept a quantity of herbs which he selected and used lavishly, wild garlic, sage and sorrel. He finely cut up all the ingredients on a flat stone with the best knife he could find.

Gradually with the addition of oatmeal and some of the congealed blood it began to look like sausage meat. He had soaked the entrails in water to keep them soft and clean and pulling them inside out and back again he cut them into shorter lengths. With a bone spoon he began stuffing the meat mixture into the skins tied at one end until about two foot was full and tied it off, then twisted it every four inches or so to make a string of sausages. Colin was really pleased with his efforts and the women were bemused and sceptical but laughed at him. It took too long for that day's meal to achieve even a few sausages but the next day, before lunch he put some of his dripping mixture into the metal tray on the fire and fried his first batch of sausages. To Colin they were bland and greasy but his friends were impressed and gathered round urging him to show them again. Colin eyed the ducks and dreamed of toad in the hole.

CHAPTER 5

WINTER SOLSTICE

Colin's calendar now had four strings, the last with 20 pieces of reddish bark. Nearly Christmas. He had got over the first wave of depression and realised he would have to actively stop thinking about his past life and wishing that he could get back. It made him sad and desperate and worse - frightened. The enormity of what was going on was too much for him to take in and it was easier to curtail his thoughts to the challenges of the present.

He had achieved his dream of cooking toad in the hole. The women were not keen to make sausages but were willing to let him have the ingredients. It was the dogs who were deprived of the offal he used. The oat flour was so coarse it did not make a good batter but he managed a rather soggy pudding crisped round the edges and it was a change from the broth and oatcakes. His success drove him on and he tried omelettes and quiche. He was stumped as to what to put in them. No onions or tomatoes, no cheddar cheese.

They made a goats cheese that was strong and sour but did not improve the quiche mix and the flattened oat mix he used to line the bronze tray he tried to bake it in did not amount to pastry. However he acquired a certain kudos for his inventiveness. The men were disturbed; cooking was women's work. To see a man cooking made them shake their heads in dismay.

There was no more salmon fishing, the fish having gone off to the sea, but Colin continued to educate himself about the waterways and found a few pools where he could guarantee a catch. He earned the right to eat with the men which meant he got to eat fish or fowl or meat every day and he began to feel stronger and leaner. As the winter progressed the weather remained chilly but not frosty. He had got used to being barefoot most of the time and only used his pattens when they had to walk anywhere. The chief's men did wear leather boots but it appeared that the killing of oxen was so rare there was not enough hide thick enough to make boots for everyone. On two occasions Colin had been taken to the chief's hall and he was tickled to see the chief wore the Hush Puppies on each occasion despite their being clearly several sizes too big. Colin gazed at them longingly. Who would have thought such a mundane item could have been coveted so dearly.

Apart from the Bard, others called at the village. A man with a young boy and two ponies came one day with panniers on one pony containing rock salt. He weighed the lumps of salt on a scale and was given a considerable amount of goods in return; a finished bow and quiver, some wool clothing, metal knife blades and was given food and shelter for the night. Clearly salt was a rare commodity saved for high days and holidays and no doubt for the chief. While the men sat round the fire and told tales of faraway places Colin, who had become used to the sound of the villager's tongue, heard the man use the word Romani. He kicked himself that he had not learned more language so that he could ask the man questions. "Did he mean Romans?" "Were they here in Britain?" or "had they travelled abroad?" Colin could hail a friend, say good morning or goodnight, praise the sun and moon and ask for a variety of foods, materials and services. He knew the proper names for everything in the village but was unable to grasp any sort of grammar that enabled him to form sentences. The visitor had been introduced to Colin at the start and was curious about his clothes and physique. He appeared to be able to give some insight into peoples of similar height and colouring which seemed to reassure them that he had simply come from another place- possibly travelling up-river and lost his boat. His ability to fish and cook in strange ways suggested he came from a tribe from far lands.

On another occasion an old man and a cart came with two youths. He brought raw wool and took finished garments away in return. He did not travel on northwards so Colin guessed he had an arrangement with another village who had excess wool and fewer weavers. He had also seen a party of merchants go along the road after stopping at the chief's hall. They did not stop in the village to sell but bought mead and ate a meal there. Colin learned that they sold imported goods and was fascinated to see their glazed crockery, pewter, and wooden boxes containing spices and jewellery. No one in the village could afford such things but Colin thought there might be larger towns where such things were bartered. He had seen no money but if he lived in Roman times there would have been currency of a sort. These visitors and their wares made him yearn to travel down the road to see the wider world. Surely there must be a town where Gloucester would one day be? Or sea ports? These merchants must have come across the sea with the goods they sold. How he desired to pack up and walk out of the village with them to explore the world.

It was only two days later he was able to explore the western road. The day before the camp was alive with preparations. A cart was brought from the smelting yard and harnessed to two oxen and the bed covered with sheepskins. Food was packed, apples and oatcakes, little saffron cakes wrapped in a wool cloth and a ram was tethered to the cart. Crocks of mead were stored on the cart and at the last the young children were lifted into the back. Everyone put on their best clothes, strapped on pattens and after a lunch of hare broth and bread they set off over a series of wooden bridges across the Severn towards the Malvern Hills. The chief's men joined them at the road, leaving behind six strong men to guard the village and the animals.

On the far side of the Severn they came upon another track that wound through rocky outcrops and marshy heaths that Colin believed was Longdon. There were plenty of large birds in the sky that eyed their cargo and the ram. Rooks, ravens and hawking birds swooped and cawed from every promontory or tree and Colin began to feel that something momentous was occurring. According to his calendar it was 21st December, the shortest day of the year. He knew that Christmas had been moved to fit in with the pagan rituals so this must be what they did at Christmas.

After four hours travelling it was getting dark already and they lit torches to show their way. Increasingly they met other parties on the road, some just families, on one occasion a convoy of three carts that came up from the south. Everyone was excited and chattering together as they walked along the tracks that were turfed and although wet, were passable. By 6 o'clock by his reckoning they reached a heath hard by the Malvern Hills which towered menacingly above them. It was new moon and the crescent stood out in a brilliant intensity just over the ridge. Despite the torchlight it was dark as pitch and the carts drew up in a rough crescent around a circle of fire. A bonfire was being lit and in its flames Colin became aware of the dark vertical shape - a single standing stone.

People arrived from every direction, making a torchlit path from the far side of the Malverns and drawing up in carts and by pony from both roads. It was cold and Colin was surprised the villagers showed no signs of being chilled. The children slept in the sheepskins on the cart and he wished he could join them. He was cold and bored. About two hours later the ceremony started. It reminded him of Guy Fawkes night; food was handed round and mead in beakers and the bonfire near the stone was stoked higher and higher until they could almost feel the warmth. After a while Colin heard an increasing sound of drums and discordant pipes and into the firelight strode the Bard he had seen in the village. This time his white robe had red wool woven into the neck and hem and he appeared wild and ferocious with his forked beard and ponytail. He roared incantations and as the drummer became faster and more insistent he swayed and whirled in time, throwing something into the fire that threw sparks and flames up into the night sky. The crowd gasped and shrieked with excitement and the children who were wrapped in blankets were brought forward to watch.

The Bard marched to and fro pointing now at the moon a silver sickle and drew forth his own golden sickle in parody. He strode around the circle shaking bunches of mistletoe at groups of people, rolling his eyes in a fearsome way and growling and gnashing in a very theatrical manner. Colin was not too impressed. He had seen too many travel programmes on TV to believe this was any more than a show for the masses. As the moon disappeared behind the hills the Bard began a whirling dance to the rhythm of the pipes and drums. He drank from a shiny goblet and invoked the Gods, throwing his robed arms skywards and dancing around the stone. A white mare was led into the circle of fire and Colin felt his first pang of emotion. It was the same ceremony as that of Halloween, but surely they would not sacrifice a horse? He watched apprehensively as the crowd drew nearer and tensed significantly but what happened next was beyond his expectations.

The mare was brought up to the standing stone, meekly it seemed and held by two men. Behind her he noticed a rock on to which the Bard suddenly leapt and to Colin's horror drew aside his robes to reveal a huge erection. He chanted, reached out his arms to the monolith and in one thrust, penetrated the mare. The crowd leaned forward with a roar and pounded the ground in the rhythm with the drums, both they and the Bard working themselves to a frenzy. Colin did not know where to look. It was worse than a pornographic film Martin had got hold of when they were fifteen.

Eventually as the crowd screamed to a crescendo the Bard screamed and leapt back from the pony who, mildly surprised, was led away. People began moving forwards and dancing to the music. The older women stayed behind with the children, but rocked in time with the drums and one turned to Colin and urged him to join in. Despite his diffidence it was hard not to look at the scene and feel moved by the pulse. The mead was running through his veins warming him and quickening his heart. He had no intention to dance or join in but he became aware of one of the village girls nearby sitting on an upturned crock staring invitingly at him. She was the brown haired girl who was always eyeing him up with her deep blue eyes who had teased and flirted with him before but now her meaning was unmistakable. She opened her legs and stroked her thighs with both hands in rhythm with the music. Colin looked round to find everyone else engaged in some tangle with another person. He tried to recall her parents; Mard and Arna, but the village was her extended family. If he had sex with this young girl would he be breaking some code of behaviour or would they kill him for it? Or worse, would he have to marry her?

In the end the decision was taken away from him. The girl stood up and came over to him and started rubbing her body against him and it was beyond him to resist. The old woman nearby laughed and waved her arm suggestively and pulling the girl into the darkness he buried himself in the mysteries of the moon goddess.

The night was long. Although the chanting and dancing went on after midnight and Colin and the girl fell asleep together having found a deerskin from the cart to lie on, they were awake and moving before dawn. Some of the men and the Bard were re-kindling the bonfire and the white mare stood by unmoved by the experience. Colin felt ashamed and embarrassed by his performance. His inexperience must have been obvious to this girl but he wondered if she had been a virgin as it had been a more aggressive struggle than he had imagined and she had cried out. He lay next to her in the dark trying to recall if any of the girls slept with the men in the village. It appeared to him that couples slept in their own huts once they had reached puberty. He had been grateful to have a place to sleep without noticing who slept with who. His three companions always came to sleep in his hut at each night. How did they choose partners? Was it on nights like this? Clearly this girl had set her sights on him as soon as he had arrived. Had she told her family and did they approve? He decided to get up and walk about to put some distance between them before people started regrouping.

At last dawn came. As the sunlight appeared to the south the people roused themselves, stood in the ceremonial area and faced the rising sun, hailing it and chanting while the Bard added his incantations. No doubt they knew the days would now grow longer, the sap rise and the life quicken beneath their feet and many of the women would bear their children conceived at this precious time. Maybe his blue eyed beauty would too. It was out of his control now.

After dawn they gathered their possessions together, put the children in the carts and slowly made their way homewards. Friends who had met up overnight said their farewells and young girls wistfully said goodbye to their night lovers. Colin began to see that this was the best way to pro-create their tribes. The intermingling would make for strong children and avoid incest occurring. Because it was conducted under the aegis of the Gods in a frenzy there was no way of knowing which male had impregnated which girl or who was responsible afterwards. Presumably the resultant babe was taken into the family regardless. This explained how the blue eyed girls had been born in a village of dark haired, brown eyed people. Colin thought briefly about the prospect of a 6' male being born into a village of men only 5'4". Presumably there was some value in height to them. Not that he could think of one. Clearly the chief chose his men who were bigger and heavier than the village people possibly because they ate all the meat. Colin's genes would give the village people better standing in future if they could engender tall men and possibly enable them to become part of the chief's clan.

But for the present he could see no value in being taller. The pallet he slept on was a foot too short for him. Squatting on logs to eat was difficult as his knees came up under his chin and did not help his digestion. He envied the elder his proper chair and wondered why they did not all have one if they could make them. In fact he could see quite a few improvements they were able to make but did not. Chairs, proper beds, wool blankets, leather shoes, dry paths and more comfortable shirts were some of the assets he thought of. He still missed onions and potatoes, hot baths and shampoo and commercial beer, but after a stew of hare and root vegetables, warm honey and oat cakes and a pint of mead to snuggle down in his sheepskin, unwashed, and to spend his days fishing, making flies and having a laugh with the village youths was good enough. In fact at times he felt he fitted in as much with them as he had at home. Colin had always been the timid sort who always wanted to do the right thing. He had never wanted to rebel or thieve or get drunk or get into trouble with the other boys and was not popular with most of his peers. Although not particularly bright he preferred reading and studying and going fishing with his father and his older friends.

His only concern now was the girl. Her name was something like Sian and he felt an unwelcome sense of responsibility for her. He regretted his descent into copulation and having no feelings for the girl herself he was perplexed as to how he was expected to carry on now. Would she want to sleep with him regularly? What would the villagers expect? Where would it happen? In front of other people like last night. No way would he manage that again. But on the journey home he noticed Sian spent much of the journey tittering and giggling with the other girls no doubt giving them a blow by blow account of his performance.

On return to the village the families returned to their huts, the village rhythm interrupted for once. By the time they got home it was lunchtime and they had another ceremony around the fire which apparently had to be re-kindled in a different place with an ember from the ritual site which had been brought in a cauldron. By the time food was on again it was getting dark. Colin had visited his eel net and found three fat eels trapped and they were welcome additions to the pot. Of the men who were left behind one had caught ducks and a swan which was a first for Colin. The celebrations made him feel almost like Christmas but the swan would take at least a day to pluck, hang and prepare and another day to cook it so it would be 24th December for the feast. Colin added another piece of bark to his December string and wondered what spring would bring.

Colin had tried hard to manage his emotions from day to day but often woke up feeling depressed. The relentless days of boredom, cold and lack of communication were getting him down. Whilst he had been quite resilient about coping practically, since his failed trip to Gloucester a deeper sense of bereavement and loss had come over him. He felt weak and helpless and memories of his old life came easily to his mind. He wondered what on earth must his family be thinking. His mother would be distraught with worry, his father angry that he had let everyone down, the bank, the Lions, his gardening work. "What was he playing at disappearing like that, telling no-one all over a silly girl at that".

He wished so much he could relieve them of this worry that must be affecting them so badly. And what sort of Christmas must they be having? He imagined Auntie Vi arriving to no decorations, no celebrations, the house dull and cold and everyone keeping a stiff upper lip. Maggie and her fellow staying out more and more to avoid the recriminations and neighbours not liking to ask too many questions. Perhaps they thought he had gone off to London in pursuit of Lesley. Nothing was less in his mind now. He thought of her as shallow and silly. How would she have coped in his situation? Had he actually liked her even? Maybe she was just approachable. He never felt comfortable with the way she dressed; those short dresses and the false eye-lashes were just unnecessary in a place like Tewkesbury. He had been chuffed to be seen out with her but not really proud of her. Last Christmas at the Swan Dance she had been flirting with Martin then she denied it but now he knew it was true. The summer before they had been to Upton with the crowd for the day and she had been quite sarcastic about him saying "prospects". Why had he not seen her as she really was?

His brother would be coming round to give his mother support. He did not think David would put him down. As a brother he had always been a support and role model to Colin. When he had been bullied at school it was David who had turned up at the school gate and threatened their leader not his Dad. Why had he taken all this for granted?

He thought about the staff in the bank. Vaughan was the chief clerk, his immediate boss. He would be furious that Colin had "gone off" just after he had done so much to get him this promotion to assistant chief clerk, at twenty three as well. Pamela the administrator was such a helpful woman, she was like another mother to him, she would be worried sick too. All these people not knowing what he was going through.

He tried to restore his mental balance by remembering good times. He had done lots of work for the Lions; carol singing at Christmas, the sponsored cross country run last summer when he had come fifth and the winner was a professional runner. He was so proud he had raised £480 on his own too. Then there was Dorothy. She had lived in the old cottages opposite the Bear. He had been doing her garden for the last three years for nothing; she made a lovely piece of ginger cake too, always a treat at the end of the day. Trevor, who was the treasurer of the Lions, was always remarking what a good person Colin was for giving up his spare time. He recalled family picnics from his childhood with boiled eggs, ham sandwiches and chicken legs, fruit cake and home made jellies. To Tintern Abbey, Upton and Ross on Wye. He used to go fishing with David down by the weir and caught his first salmon when he was sixteen and took it back for tea. He had had salmon sandwiches for school for days. School; that was a happy place for him. He had worked hard and found it easy to pass exams. The boys who were disruptive were put in a separate class at fifteen where they just painted the school and did the grounds, if they came to school at all, leaving him and his friends to get on with studying. He had felt so superior to these boys but he knew deep down that they did not have the start in life he did. How would he have coped without a Dad or a nice home and a car and holidays. How would they have coped in his place now?

Maybe all his life had been leading to this? He had not believed in fate, ever, but somehow his belief that you got what you earned had been shattered now. He thought he had done everything right but he had ended up looking a fool and being rejected. Was it some sort of punishment for being proud of what he had achieved?

No one could prepare for being catapulted into another century, even astronauts believed they would be coming home eventually. His submissiveness had allowed the villagers to see him as unthreatening. His politeness had allowed the chief to take his belongings off him. If he had been more aggressive he could be dead by now. His inventiveness and practicality had allowed him to find ways of helping the tribe, like being in the Lions.

His education had allowed him to recognise where he was and to make some sense of the wider context of living in the iron age. A less kind person might have been rejected by the village and stoned to death. A less useful person might have been less well looked after. A less educated person might have panicked and tried to attack his hosts. Certainly his qualities had allowed him, for at least three months, to survive. In three days they had hung and plucked the swan ready for a feast. Colin was not sure if the chief had other people catching food as he had only had a venison and a boar in the last two months but presumably expected more as it was winter. Colin missed greens, oddly enough, especially as he hated cabbage, but leeks and Brussels sprouts, green beans and peas were things he craved now. Nettles were the only green thing available at this time of year and they were used plentifully in soups and stews. Once they had set aside a day for feasting on the swan they also killed a sheep and there was roast fowl and lamb for everyone for three days. Mead was given to all the elders and a rough, hot cider, with froth on top for everyone else. They sat up listening to stories after dark with their rough blankets pulled up over their heads. A minstrel of sorts appeared that day and played something like bag-pipes and a drum and there was dancing and singing too. Although he could not join in Colin felt far more festive than he would watching Sunday Night at the London Palladium or Rowan and Martin's Laugh In. The dark haired girl was there as well and she came and sat on his log offering him mead from a pottery jar. He had not felt so warm and included before and he was delighted when she let him put his arm round her and kiss her. The mead was going to his head. Although honey flavoured it was strong, more like whisky and the smoke from the fires and the heady music and dancing increased his feeling of being drunk. The next thing she was leading him away to somewhere indoors. He vaguely recognised his own bed and before long he was engulfed in the warmth and muskiness of his animal skins.

Colin had not considered that he could enjoy sex with anyone at any time and without the girl's parent's approval. It simply had not occurred to him that such a young girl would be independent. The tribe seemed very moral and religious in broad terms but he could not get his head around the free love that seemed to exist. He was aware that most people were in couples but if so why were the other three males sleeping in the communal tent?

Sian got up and left before they came back. Colin slept the sleep of the just and blameless. When he awoke he was mildly dismayed that she was not at his side but could she be naked in front of three other men? After the orgy at Malvern he was prepared to expect anything but in the village there was not exactly promiscuity. He began to think of her as his woman and certainly if he thought she would sleep with anyone else he could be prepared to fight, provided they did not use a sword. It was not necessary, fortunately. As far as he could see she slept in her family home every night under the watchful eyes of her parents and submitted to him alone.

CHAPTER 6

THE GIRL

Soon after he added the last piece of bark to the December string on his calendar it became significantly colder. While it was not yet freezing Colin realised he must do something to get warmer clothing. He had taken one of his sheepskins from the bed and made arm holes and wore it over his sweater but even this was becoming inadequate once he stopped moving around. On some days he went with the younger boys to the smelting grounds and was welcomed now as a bellows worker. This job seemed to be the province of younger boys who in turns worked the bellows all day. Colin found that not only did he keep warmer but he was building some muscle in his upper body too. Never before had he felt the value of his own flesh when he worked in the bank but since he started participating in local life he realised his strength and agility were paramount. Even to fish and collect food they walked long distances. He had to climb down banks of the river in places and was often expected to carry large quantities of wood, kindling and brushwood from the forests that now covered most of what would one day be Gloucestershire.

About three miles away in a clearing, close up against Prestbury Hill, was an encampment of charcoal burners. All around the woods had been coppiced and with metal headed axes they cut the 1 ½" stems of hazel boughs to make up the great stands of wood covered in turves that smouldered for days. The warm charcoal was loaded into willow baskets and that the men carried on their backs, the load being light for the quantity, but Colin being the tallest was always required to carry the heavy wood for the fires. Now it was winter the fires were kept going all day; the younger people sat out still before retiring after dark, but he noticed the older people stayed in their huts for much of the time, only coming out for the rising sun ceremonies. He was invited into the girl's family's hut one dark and drizzly day soon after New Year and was impressed how homely it was.

The couple, whom he called Mard and Arna, as best he could pronounce it, had three other children all about six or seven, and a grandmother. Their beds were alongside the curved turf walls of the hut and in the centre a large hearth smouldered with charcoal giving a smokeless glowing warmth to the room. Arna was one of the weavers and her loom stood by the door, it's smooth pebble loom weights familiar to Colin's eye from visits to museums.

Apart from sheepskins the family did have blankets died in ochre yellow and red shades and woven reed baskets and platters and pillows of goose down. Mard's spears and nets for hunting hung on the walls. No doubt the discomfort in the men's huts was due to a value for Spartan conditions to harden them up but not a lack of skill or imagination.

Colin began to wonder how he could barter for some of these comforts -another feather pillow, rough as it was, would help him get through the long nights. And was there any reason he could not make his bed longer so he could at least lie stretched out and keep his feet warm too?

Of course there was a down side to comfort. Increasingly Colin found himself itching and scratching and it soon dawned on him that lice were unavoidable. He took to shaving both his head and beard despite the cold, and weekly washed his own shirt in the icy brown water of the river, beating it on an outcrop of stone at the bend in the watercourse and searching for lice when the daylight was strongest. There seemed no element that could kill them so he resigned himself to obsessive nit picking whenever he had a spare moment. Although the men did not shave he was able to fashion an iron blade sharp enough to make a makeshift razor that he kept sharp by honing it on a smooth stone. He knew razors were familiar to them because the bard had a partly shaven head and cheeks. The villagers looked at him curiously when he had shaved both his head and face but were not perplexed and no doubt assumed it was a tribal affectation from wherever he had come.

Since the travelling salesman had come he hankered after another trip away from the village. All these travellers must be coming and going at a day's ride at least from somewhere to somewhere. They were selling plenty of goods and bartering other goods to sell and if only he could ask them they would tell him what lay ahead. Whilst no one seemed likely to stop him leaving he felt it was impolite to stop his chores after the hospitality they had shown him and he could not verbalise his wishes or intentions either. He contented himself by building an extension to his bed, asking for some rough sacking type material to make a bigger pallet and collected some dry grass to fill it. He had wanted straw but in winter fodder and bedding for the ox and ponies in the corral seemed in short supply. No doubt one took straw in July at the harvest to make extra beds.

Colin had been keeping an eye on Sian after the night of the feast and she had returned to her parents' hut as if nothing had happened. In the following weeks she often cast him a knowing smile but his fears that she would expect a commitment were unfounded. Once he was relieved of the sense of commitment to her he began to let his senses run wild and began hoping for a repeat performance. First he started returning her smile and let his gaze follow her about the camp. She, like her mother, was involved in the clothing production, carded and spun the wool her mother wove and stitched garments with a bone needle. He watched her cross-legged before the firelight, the soft wool across her lap, glowing in the red light of the flames and remembered over and over the muscular roundness of her thighs and breasts and how she had instinctively responded to him, despite his clumsiness. Did they teach their children what to do? She seemed all knowing and well-practiced in her coupling compared to him who had had no more experience than fumbled petting in the back of his car. He wanted very much to practice his technique now but the rhythm of the camp seemed such a fixed pattern he was unsure how to instigate a meeting. In the third week of January, when the weather was at its coldest, he saw her leaving her mother's hut and walk towards the sheep hands where her younger brother was a shepherd boy. He followed. The raised ground above the river bed, where Tewkesbury High Street would one day run with its building societies, pubs and shops, was dotted about with hawthorn brakes and hummocks so that one could gain some cover and privacy. He felt awkward following her but after 100 yards he sat down on a tussock to see if she would return that way and allow herself to be waylaid. Her brother, whilst watching the sheep, gathered little tufts of sheep's wool from the briars and while she had taken out some bread and ewes cheese to him she returned with the collected wool wrapped within her shawl.

Colin, at a loss, stayed sitting on the tussock, fearing that if he stood he might intimidate her by his height. Sure enough she returned across the meadow with her small bundle of wool and slowed as she approached him. She smiled and her eyes were mischievous. Stopping to talk and flirt, a habit quite wasted on him, he noticed her glance flashed between the village and the sheep as she gauged how visible they were from either view. Colin held out his hand encouraging her to come to him and she willingly stood against him, welcoming his hands on her. He immediately felt aroused remembering the passion with which they had tumbled in his hut.

After some teasing she put her fingers on his lips and indicated she would kiss him and spread her legs over his lap as he drew her towards him. Now he felt he would brave all her brothers and father to have her again and cautiously stood up drawing her behind a hawthorn thicket. She obligingly threw down her shawl in the rank grass and they clutched inexpertly at each other. This time she was less desperate and made him wait longer, sitting astride him while she guided his hands where she wanted them. In the distance the shepherd boys were occupied together and their gaze did not turn towards the village. No one came up from the village either. Colin reminded himself in this brief respite, that lovemaking was supposed to be an anticipated and drawn out affair in order to give most pleasure but as an inexpert lover his body took over his reasoning and he was soon gasping with surprise that it was all over already. He was disappointed with himself and while in his old life there was nowhere comfortable or private to make love here there were no boundaries at all and he still could not get it right. He felt aggrieved that as he could not communicate in words he had no way of knowing how to get his own hut or the right to sleep with this girl. She on the other hand was now rocking her body and the insistent rhythm effected the desired repeat performance, this time less hurried with Colin on top where he felt more in control and able to relish the subtleties of different movements of the girl's pelvis, the texture of her flesh and the rising of her emotion.

Colin began to think of himself as a lover. He was delighted to see that she glowed with pink cheeks and red lips as the result of his endeavours and looked radiant and happy. Would he have been able to make Lesley look like that? Why had he always held back? No wonder she had been disappointed in him if this was what women wanted. After Sian had tripped back to the village, smiling to herself, Colin decided he would have to make some overture to her father to see if they could formally be paired together. Now he had tasted satisfaction he could not imagine forgoing it again as long as he lived and breathed.

Colin had added 122 pieces of bark to his calendar and thought they had now passed New Year, when he was awoken in the middle of the night by the hunters. It was pitch dark. Initially he feared they would be attacked and he expected he would have to fight, but no weapons were produced. They shouted to him to get up and get dressed, and by the time he was ready a large crowd had gathered outside the huts. It was clearly something of great importance as the women and children were all dressed too and exited. His glance immediately fell on Sian whose shining eyes made him want to run to her now, pick her up and run off with her. However the hunters were now doing some sort of ritual dance around the fire. They danced and sang and painted each other's faces in the firelight with red and white ochre. Their beards were covered in whitish clay and their weapons were brandished, bow and spear. Colin sat fascinated but at the back of his mind he began to worry if this was another boar hunt? Had someone seen one close by? A boar feast in mid-winter would be very popular with the chief and his men. But the atmosphere was different. No one danced and painted their faces when they went to the boar; they were singing and chanting as if getting their courage together, but there had been no rituals like this one. Three of the elders were wrapped in furs and conducting the ceremony and after anointing the hunters with red ochre and giving them some sort of potion, the head elder produced a sort of leather bag and presented it to the lead hunter. The bag was slowly opened for the crowds to see and inside Colin could see, glittering by the firelight, a mass of gold fibres, that reminded him of his grandmothers hairnet. It was delicately pulled from the bag and unrolled for the crowd's delight who cheered and chanted as the lead hunter displayed their prize. Colin still did not know what it was. It was a net, something like five feet across, stiff looking and wiry, and it was not until he pushed nearer to firelight that he realised it was made of strands of gold knitted together. He could not imagine what it was for; no boar would be held by such a delicate mesh. Nor any other animal he could think of neither hares nor squirrels.

After about an hour of rituals the hunters headed off to the forest and the crowd loosely following behind. The girls were gossiping and admiring the hunters and Colin caught Sian around the waist. To his disappointment she was more interested in following the hunt than disappearing with him and took his hand and led him forwards to the edge of the trees. Soon he was commandeered by the hunters and given a stick and sent, with two other men, round behind a thicket to wait. It was still pitch dark, no moon tonight, but the sparkling stars gave a little ghostly light to see that the hunters were crouching some way off with their gilded net hung in a gap between the trees. Colin could see on the distant horizon to the east the faintest edge of light creeping up in a gold beam and one hunter gave a silent signal to the others. He and the two others began beating the bushes before them and moving towards the hunters. It was hard as bramble and thorn tore at his legs and he could see neither path nor obstacle. He was aware that from other directions other beaters were also closing inwards focussing on the net in the centre.

Colin was still perplexed. He was aware such tactics were used to beat up pheasants from undergrowth but not at night and certainly not with a single net. And as far as he had seen there were no pheasants in the woods anyway. Eventually he became aware his companion drawing in his breath through his teeth as if in great consternation and he felt a shiver of fear run down his spine like ice cold water. What was so frightening? He heard the chatter and alarm call of small birds flying through the bushes. He knew the sound but it was some seconds before he realised they were wrens. Dozens of the little birds were fluttering from bush to bush confused by the beaters approaching from every direction and sure enough they were soon fluttering and shrieking, caught by the golden net that was by now taught between the trees. The hunters snatched at the birds as their feet and wings became entangled in the wire and quickly dispatched them, some falling to the ground and some remaining hanging from the net. But Colin still could not understand why they would want to catch and kill wrens. Surely they were far too tiny to eat and why such complex ritual?

By the rise of the sun they had caught something like a hundred birds and each one was ceremonially picked up and tied carefully on poles and transported above their heads.

On leaving the woods the villagers and now some of the soldiers from the camp were all cheering and shouting with glee. They made their way along the edge of the forest to the standing stones where everyone stood around the edges of the circle to watch. This time a priest, not the wizard he had seen at the Malverns, but the priest from the chiefs camp, was waiting with his ceremonial sickle, his white cape and boots. The hunters brought to him the gold net, now devoid of the tiny captives and he performed the purification ceremony with oils dispersed by a bunch of herbs in his hand and by a flame on a taper of wax. He passed the flame through, across and around before eventually it was returned to its ceremonial leather pouch and given back to the chief elder.

The sun had risen as they watched and now the horizon pink and red, streaked through, brought them back to the real world. Sian had moved across the groups and was now nestling into his side. Colin knew there would be no barrier to sex this time and for the first time began to feel how the pace and performance of the rituals could be a prelude to sex. Clearly they believed their ceremonies were powerful and essential to their survival and were undertaken to provoke the generative forces. Sian no doubt believed that any offspring created would be blessed and protected, healthier and stronger. After an hour in a mossy hollow with her, oblivious to the cold, he could not wait until the next ritual performance. He worked out on his calendar this must be the equivalent of St Valentine's Day although he thought that was a Victorian invention. He could see they feared and despised the wrens by their vituperative treatment of them. In the stone circle they had been tied to poles, their wings outstretched on skewers and left. The next day Colin went to see in daylight the black hazel poles with their tiny crucified victims, but he could think of no one reason to pick on this one harmless bird. He wished he could speak enough of their language to ask but while he felt confident greeting people, sharing food, asking for raw materials and whispering to Sian, complex philosophical discussions were beyond him.

It was shortly after the wren hunt that he began to notice the days were lengthening. The cloudy darkness that came at three or four in winter was now nearer five or later by his reckoning. There did not seem to be any measure of time known to these people but nor was there any reason to have. They were so in touch with the weather and the seasons that they all knew what would happen at each change of the moon or stars. They bore with the cold and wet knowing that before long the spring and summer would come back again. Throughout the early part of the year, despite the central bonfire they spent weeks indoors unless they were working. Even the openings where Arna had kept her loom were covered in old blankets on a wooden frame, shutting out much of the daylight. When the weak winter sun arose she took advantage of it and sat among the others of the womenfolk outside their huts carding wool, but their days were short and much of the work got done indoors by rush lights.

The end of February saw snow and the little brown sheep brought nearer the camp and corralled. This was when the fodder collected throughout the year and kept dry under weighted nets was used up. Hay, straw, peas and all manner of dried greenstuffs he did not recognise were collected in the hot summer months and stacked under thatches of reeds. Many of the sheep were killed in autumn, that year's rams, bar one or two, their fleeces used for wool, bedding, coats and shoes, rugs and harness. Their meat was sent up to the chief's camp and the offal kept for the villagers. Colin had once seen a film of Scots people making haggis. He knew you used the sheep's stomach and minced up the offal with oatmeal and spices. He attempted one with Sian's mother, Arna, but was at a loss what to use for spices. He cut up the liver, heart and tongue as finely as possible, mixed it with oats and ground up in a mortar and added a pinch of the precious salt, some wild sage he recognised in the brakes and some sorrel they kept dried in winter. It still tasted pretty drab once boiled but made a change from the usual stew and occasional roasted meat they were used to. They still recalled his sausage making exploits from the winter and laughed and joked as they watched his latest culinary experiment. Despite this the sausages had been a success although there was no pork meat available in winter. Although the Great River Severn kept flowing there was very little fishing available and the creeks and gullies that bred elvers and minnows in summer were frozen solid. They either died or grew into bigger fish who waited sluggishly at the bottom of the river waiting for spring and the supply of flying insects and larva on which they thrived.

Colin could think of no benefits to winter here. In later years people would learn to skate and sledge and at least get some fun out of the ice and snow. Here it was just a period of hindrance and famine that required patience to get through. He wondered if they knew there were other countries in the south that had no winter and if they knew would they choose to move? There were still activities going on in the camp. In the short daylight hours the hunters still went out but their success was greater in the bare woods and clear background. They returned twice with a red deer, occasionally hares and numerous types of wildfowl that presumably wintered here from the arctic. Colin recognised teal and woodcock as well as geese and swans. There was another bird, almost turkey like that lived on the moorland on top of the hills. There were so many people to feed though that everything had to be stretched a long way and any major prizes always went to feed the chief and his men first. The villagers would get back a leg of venison with the offal or boars trotters or the skins of hares after the men had eaten the best pieces. One goose that was plucked jointed, gutted and boiled with some fennel, barley and turnips fed the whole village. Morsels of goose meat were kept for children and the elderly when the pot cooled by early morning the goose fat skimmed off and kept in earthenware pots for basting leaner meats and even for fuel for rush lights. The beaks were honed into sharp blades set in wood handles for skinning and cutting food, the feathers made into pillows and the tiny bones were split for marrow and used as needles. The coloured wing and tail feathers were kept for use in ceremonies as headgear or small brushes for sweeping indoors. Not one item of any animal was thrown away and even the scaly feet were used to feed the odd piglet left to grow throughout the winter.

Colin had plenty of time on his hands. Some of the older men played board games and gambling games with bone or stone counters and boards made of hide. Without speech he had some difficulty getting the rules but something like draughts was fairly simple. Another game reminded him of snakes and ladders but had straight tracks to go down and was easy to understand. There were five sorts of counters in different colours-black, grey, greenish grey, pinkish grey and white. Chunky stones with colours painted on each side were used like dice. Depending on which colour fell upright that colour counter could move across the board. The counters getting to the top of the board first were the winners and Colin was not sure how but he got enough of the gist of it to join in. He thought it would be a good project to make a chess set, board and pieces and started to plan how he could fashion it out of available fabrics.

The chief elder of the village, Yoan, who carried out the rituals of death, sunrise, sunset and the minor changes of the moon also carried rune stones. Colin recognised them immediately from a history lesson and he had had a pouch of five which came free with a serial magazine. These were flat, small pebbles with a symbol in white on each thrown at the behest of anyone with a question, a problem or a wish.

"Will my wife get pregnant this spring?"

"Should we hunt today?"

"Help my husband recover from his chesty cough"

"Let the spring come early and unfreeze the meres"

"Give my son a long and healthy life"

There was no point in Colin joining in as he had no idea what the priest was telling him. "When can I go back to my own time?" was prevalent in his mind but also "will I have a life with my girl here" was beginning to creep into his mind. However one day the priest did beckon to him and indicate he should put his hand on the pouch the stones were kept in. He cast them on a soft cloth of yellow wool and Colin stared uncomprehendingly at the white signs. The priest looked and rubbed his chin, hummed a bit, then with both hands patted his chest and sides, smiling and nodding. Colin took this to mean he would enjoy good health. The priest pointed at three rune stones that had fallen apart from the others and with his right hand pointed up and over into the distance. Whether this meant a long life or a long journey he did not know. But a long journey was not something he had envisaged.

The only trade that seemed to flourish in winter was smelting. Ponies laden with ore trudged across the wooden bridge bringing iron ore to the site. The ore was thrown into the ovens filled with charcoal, kept hot with bellows, and a constant supply of fuel. After several hours of intense heat and careful covering and testing eventually the molten iron trickled out of a small spout at the base of the oven into clay beakers that were held with wooden tongs that were quickly used to pour it into clay moulds already prepared. After a few minutes cooling the clay moulds were broken and the dagger or sword or scythe blade was revealed and then beaten against a smooth boulder and reheated in another brazier until the metal was honed to sharpness. Colin loved standing in the shelters with the fires blazing, blackening his face and warming his body. Somehow he had got used to never feeling warm even in bed and he was reluctant to go back to the village. He picked up a little skill at iron work too as the workers were pleased to let him into their workshop to beat the iron as his greater height and weight allowed him to be more thorough. He could see the repeated beating cooling and heating did not just shape the blades but also strengthened them. Some of the blades were not just moulded but different types of metal were braided together and the woven metal heated into an indestructible mesh. An army that had the best blades lasted longest in battle.

Another warming activity was swordplay. The villagers did not own swords although most had a dagger of sorts, but the village men were expected to be able to fight, presumably in case of attack from outside and used the prepared swords for their practice. Colin found he was hopeless at this sport. He was not an aggressive man by any means and in spite of his much longer reach and swing he was much too slow and unmotivated to win a fight. Maybe if he lived in a world where sword play meant life or death he would have developed these talents early in life. Quite often in practice his sheepskin jerkin was cut and nicked by his opponents' swords but it did not trigger the fighting spirit in him.

In the evenings by firelight the men wove fishing nets out of twine, carved animal bone for knife handles, sharpened their tools and processed their hides with bone tools. While doing so the priest, the elders or a travelling salesman would tell stories, sing songs or play on crude instruments. One week a herb seller with a young boy stopped a few days. He carried dried herbs not frequent in that area and potions made from them. They were not the usual sage, nettle and sorrel but rare items the elders of the village knew how to use. The older women sniffed and prodded his wares and stocked up on items that were said to aid childbirth, kill pain and heal fungal infections. Colin recognised nothing other than some dried toadstools but wished he had a potion to kill lice instantly. He prayed he would not ever need their medicines himself. It had not occurred to him what would happen if he became ill. Oddly, despite the cold no one seemed to suffer from colds or flu and the chest problems suffered by the elderly seemed more to be to do with sitting so near the wood fires for years or inhaling noxious substances during their rituals involving pipes. He supposed people just put up with headaches. Stomach problems were more apparent. Colin was aware that human worms were quite prevalent right up to the 19th century and as there was no cure he assumed people also suffered. One or two women looked so emaciated he guessed they had tape worms from the pigs and children were not cleaned or treated so he supposed they passed worms from one to another. He was always careful to eat food that had come straight from the pot or the fire and that had not been touched by other people's hands. Skin, teeth and hair problems were rife. Most people seemed to lose teeth in middle age but by then they looked pretty brown and grubby. The lack of anything sweet other than scarce honey was keeping them healthy but the flour and oats they ground in millstones was full of grit which wore down the surfaces of the teeth so that as they got older nerves were exposed and rotted away. There were forms of alopecia, possibly due to infection by lice and ticks, but in general their hair was matted and thin. He supposed their diet was pretty unbalanced and the sort of foods that kept skin and hair healthy in his former life, zinc, iron and vitamins were largely absent throughout the winter.

The herbalist took weapons, blades, bone handles, wool and cloth and precious stones that had rolled down from the welsh hills as polished pebbles in return for his potions. He stayed a few days, his boy assistant playing a deep noted wooden pipe while he told his stories by the glow of the charcoal brazier. In the heat of the family huts to which he was invited, chewing on a piece of dried pork belly, listening to the rhythm of the storyteller and the entranced faces of the listeners, Colin almost began to feel himself at home.

CHAPTER 7

DEATH CEREMONIES

Colin was beginning to get used to the bitter cold of February and having fashioned a sheepskin hat which he indicated to his room mates they were not to try on, managed to keep his stubbly, nit free head warm. Somehow his feet, in wool bindings and pattens, seemed not to trouble him anymore and when out walking he kept his hands inside the sheepskin jerkin and walked as briskly as his footwear allowed. Daily he went to the smelting yard and pumped the bellows for maybe 30 minutes at a time, making him sweat. The youths took it in turns and he had to fight them off from wearing his sheepskin hat. Colin could think of nothing worse than getting lice in it and having to put up with the eternal itching.

The sheep were still penned while the frost was hard and the fodder began getting thin and poor. Even the huntsmen were going further and further afield to find food and with the gullies largely frozen over his fishing skills were useless.

On some days they ate only hot water with yesterdays bones and gristle to flavour and oats with a few herbs added. He was intrigued to find that the tribespeople did get colds as well, sniffing and sneezing and taking to their beds as necessary. Inevitably the weather took its toll on the elderly.

One afternoon at dusk when everyone was called to the setting sun ceremony the camp elder did not appear and several people went to his hut before it was made clear he was ailing. Colin was asked to go in and look, presumably in case his tribe knew more about chest problems and it was clear to Colin he had pneumonia. His chest wheezed and whistled like an organ and his breath was shallow and his temperature high. All Colin could think of was old black and white movies where consumptives gasped their last in Victorian bedrooms. However he did suggest sitting the old man upright, keeping him warm and giving him lots of hot liquids. Despite the good intentions the man soon died. Colin was humbled that they had asked for his help and indicated that he wanted to say goodbye as Yoan lay dying. In his own world Colin had two grandparents still, as far as he knew, and had not witnessed death first hand. Seeing the ancient face sunken and lifeless and hearing the rattle of the old chest made him link himself to his own mortality. How would he die? Of some obscure pagan disease, easily treated in the twentieth century? He stroked the old man's hands, like great dry claws they seemed. Colin could see how the tribespeople thought of the ancestor being transformed into animals or birds. Slowly the old man passed away. The herbswoman pronounced him dead two days later. They set up a wail which brought all those in the camp to the outside of his hut and sat down in their grief, whimpering and weeping as the mood took them. Colin wondered if he had particular family here as all the village seemed smitten with grief. Did they see themselves as one great family all bound together with blood ties?

The women, once the initial grief was shed, began preparing the body, by washing and grooming the hair and beard. The following night the priest appeared from the chief's camp and the man's body was brought out, loosely covered in a mantle of wool; his bow, long unused, beside him and a spear across his body. The body was brought out of the hut on a stretcher carried by four men, one at each corner and, headed by the priest there gathered a procession of mourners joined by the chief's retinue and eventually the chief himself. Slowly they wound their way up to the stone circle with torches and rush lights, chanting and crying but without music.

Colin wondered if they would set a pyre and burn the body but after some purification rituals, incantations to the stars and about an hour of ceremony and rhetoric the old man's body was removed from his bier and laid in the centre of the stone circle where all his clothes were removed and his wrists and ankles staked into the ground with wooden staves and bindings. This disturbed Colin quite a bit. He could not see the purpose of the staking if they were going to burn him. Were they afraid his spirit would escape? Eventually the naked corpse and the priest were alone in the stone circle and the priest waved his switch of branches for the last time and pulled a cowl over his head and ushered the crowds away. They all bowed their heads, covered their eyes and filtered out between the twin stones at the entrance and back to the hall and village. Colin looked behind a couple of times as he walked, expecting to see some ghost or ephemera leaving the body but he was chided by his neighbour not to look back. He thought it must be unlucky.

Three days later another old woman gave up the struggle and a similar ceremony prevailed. As they processed up the beaten track to the stone circle in the flickering lights Colin thought he could see the old man's corpse in the centre, still staked out, but where his face had been was a terrible mask of skin and bone, shredded and bloodless. Where the eyes had been were empty sockets and the limbs torn apart. Suddenly Colin realised what was happening. Once exposed the corpse would attract all manner of predators to feast on the fresh meat and hawks would peck the bones, ravens peck out the eyes and tongue and wild animals attack the limbs. The stakes must secure the tough joints at the metatarsals and metacarpals, preventing the animals taking away the body parts, at least initially. And this was more than just disposing of rotting flesh, he felt. Somehow he sensed that as the body was consumed the people believed that the body, the strength and the spirit of the man went with the creatures so that he would live on as a wolf or boar or raven. A more noble destiny than a cold rotting grave.

Two more elderly people died that month. All were given their due ceremony and returned to whence they came; badger, rat or harrier, their flesh was gradually torn away from their sinews, their organs devoured and every edible scrap removed by increasingly smaller predators, worms, ants, beetles, until the bones also started to be taken. Colin, despite the gore, was fascinated to know how soon this process took place. He wanted to go every day to see how fast the process took place but instinctively knew this would be taboo. No one appeared to go near the stone circle, unless the priest undertook some specific task and he felt unable to simply to go and gawp at the dereliction of now four bodies in varying states of decay.

He was surprised then, that in four weeks time, which according to his bark calendar, which he had started afresh from what he called the first of January, leaving one blue pebble to represent 1971, was the 15th March and the clan was preparing for another ceremony. As usual the chanting around the fire, face painting with mud and the men drinking excessive quantities of mead. The chief's men appeared, this time bringing gifts of mead and venison, and joined in the ceremony. Several of the elders produced linen cloths in rolls and as the procession went again to the stone circle the priest joined them carrying a bronze dagger. Colin rather hoped it would be a rousing ceremony which pre-empted a sexual frenzy, but the whole clan seemed subdued this time. They spread out round the outside of the stone circle shouting in mourning voices. This night it was full moon and in the frosty air Colin could sense a different mood amongst them.

The priest stood before them, solemn and vocal. He talked long and loud, clearly giving a sermon on death. Colin wished so much he could understand the words. What knowledge he would gain. No one in Britain in 1971 knew exactly what was done in prehistoric times. Here he was, sole witness to the past.

He was almost holding his breath waiting for the outcome. The priest preached and challenged the people. This is death; see what awaits you all. Value the life you have and revere those who have gone beyond into the spirit world. Colin felt it very reminiscent of native American folklore. The priest with his long braided hair and leather tunic looked much as an Indian chief and the cadence of his speech was similar. Soon he raised his knife to the moon and purified it's blade in the flames of the bonfire set in front of the gates to the circle. He then moved forward to where, some distance away, the four corpses lay emaciated or bare boned. The elders followed with their linen cloths. Carefully and with great reverence the priest cut between the sinews and joints of the bodies, releasing the bones and detaching them from the stakes. The bones that remained were wrapped carefully in the linen cloths, the skulls being carried separately. Only three skulls remained. Few of the bones were unscathed. Mammals had managed to crack the big bones for their marrow, yet each was lovingly transferred to the shrouds and carried away. Once all the bones were gathered up the crowd, in two routes around the outside of the stone circle began moving into the woods beyond, towards Prestbury Hill. It was some walk, especially in the night, through the woods, but a broad path was ahead, evident in the bushes and brambles and they followed the priest and elders for over an hour to a bare piece of ground beneath the hills' shadow. There in the centre was a great turf-covered mound, surrounded by a deep ditch and ridge. At one end of the elliptical barrow were three flat stones making a complicated entrance through which the priest entered. He performed some ceremony of "opening" ritual, whereby he stroked the stones with his rod and called out to the dead within, but eventually the bones in their linen wrappings and the separate skulls were placed within the barrow. A further ceremony of closing the entrance was performed and signalled the end of the night's activities and the people walked pensively back to the village. Colin noticed that the biting cold and bitterness of the wind had subsided in this night under the stars and realised that at last spring must be with them. It might have been around midnight when he finally snuggled down into his sheepskin bed.

The following day a weak sun appeared at dawn and after the sun greeting ritual people began stirring for their usual tasks. Colin went to the river for his rapid wash and shave, much to the amusement of some of the younger children, came back and decided it was no longer necessary to wear his sheepskin hat. Although the sun had little warmth it was encouraging psychologically. He thought about his life at home, so far away it seemed, yet this camp must have been all but a quarter of a mile from where his parents' home would one day stand. Now he felt more part of this tribe with some connection with their rituals and daily routines he was more able to think about his old life without becoming so depressed.

"If I get back how will this change me?" he thought. "For starters I will never take for granted heating, lighting and a comfortable bed, or shoes and socks. Secondly I will relish bacon and sausages, toast without grit, Sunday lunch and chocolate. I'll go down the pub with a different attitude, get in a car with reverence and make love differently altogether". He also thought there were far more positives to learn as well. He came to see that much of modern culture is futile; clocks, time, being enslaved by work and people's views about yourself-how pointless. He could even see how shallow Lesley had been to be impressed by a guitar player who went to London. And about death and marriage. If it benefited the tribe to spread their genes by mating at ritual gatherings what was so important about monogamy? Why did modern man get so wound up wanting to bring up only his biological child? Did it matter? Was there more to death than just rotting away? Why did these people revere each process and take such care with the remaining parts? These people revered elders for their wisdom not their age. Their leaders were their strongest and their tallest fighters yet everyone was valued for their skills and contribution however slight.

He found no aggression here. Children fought sometimes but were not scolded or beaten, the people were very placid on the whole; no one had abused him or forced him to do anything he did not want to do. They were fascinated and curious about his differences, had a laugh at him sometimes but he had always been invited to participate in activities, not ordered. He began to wonder what happened to people who did misbehave; it was so frustrating not being able to talk to others. He vowed that if he returned to the twentieth century he would learn other languages.

Once the sun spent more time in the sky and the pools unfroze Colin spent more time setting his nets and making flies for his rod. Soon the salmon would start coming up river and they would eat like kings again. The sheep were beginning to give birth to tiny chocolate coloured lambs and the new grass peeping up through the soil was clipped short immediately by the flock. Sian's brother was often out in the scrubland minding the sheep and Sian came to gather more loose wool and bring him oatcakes. Colin took advantage of her separation from the family and despite the cold they had many encounters in the tussocks, behind hawthorn and holly. Sian tried to teach him more words, parts of the body, clothing, feelings. He told her his words for those things and they laughed at the mimes with which they communicated. At the end of the month she sought him out and drew him to her but not for sex. Patting her stomach she made a rocking movement with her arms. Suddenly he realised she was indicating she was pregnant by him. He felt hot and cold all at once and felt speechless and gave her a hug. He was not sure what this meant. No one had indicated they should not have sex, quite the opposite, but would they have to get married? He pointed at her and himself, crossed his fingers as if to show bound together. She did not understand but looked pleased and took his hand. They walked back to her parents' hut where Arna, as usual, was at her loom and obviously knew her daughter had told him. She at least was smiling and invited him in for herb tea and honey cakes. She and Sian talked incessantly and when Mard returned at dusk it was clear he also needed to say a good deal about the forthcoming baby. After taking Colin's arm and going outside he pointed at their hut and made big arm gestures as if putting up posts and weaving. Eventually Colin cottoned on that he was talking about building a new hut. Colin was delighted-surely this meant Sian and he were recognised as a couple and were eligible to have their own house?

Colin had two strings of bark for the new year finished and twenty on the third string. His wall of the hut was beginning to look decorated. In addition he had picked up all sorts of different feathers and stuck them in around his Calendar and it resembled a native American tee pee. The other three laughed at him. Presumably there were quite strong gender boundaries already in tribes, making pretty pictures out of feathers was a woman's prerogative. He thought he would decorate his new home with Sian. Clearly the baby's needs would come first, warmth and lack of draughts. He had studied the inside of the huts and noted that although the mud, hair and straw daub was thick on the outside and more or less weatherproof, inside it was dried out and crumbly. It was not good to touch or poke at it as a hole appeared and thereby a draught. They stuck moss into the holes and the older huts were brown and fuzzy inside from endless repairs. He could see why, when someone old died the hut could be knocked down or at least dismantled and the poles used again.

He was not surprised when he noticed some young men dismantling a corral and moving it to higher ground and collecting all the artefacts, straw and sticks from the area next to the mill stream. Older men were repairing the "jetty" that ran across the stream to the ham and putting new twine around the posts. He supposed this was an annual spring task but one morning he awoke to a very familiar sight. He was woken by the chatter of his fellow hunters in the dark. They were getting up for the sun ceremony but stood in the doorway pointing. It was now warm enough not to need a brazier in the hut itself and Colin got up to see what they were discussing.

As he looked over their shoulders he was aware of the great dark expanse of water that now lapped at the edge of their village. There was little light from the stars and as far as he could see the black water, flat and calm, stretched away, silent and endless. Suddenly they were inundated. Colin had no fear. The great melt of the welsh mountains came every year and flooded the Ham, usually in a very short space of time and often at night. In the day it had been marsh and tussocks; now a lake spreading for miles. In Colin's time, the hams were cultivated and flat, but the tree line of the Severn and Avon stood out with alders and willows, half submerged.

Colin wondered how this would change village life. The sheep were grazed up on the higher ground so would not go short of grass, but the pools and gullies where he caught his eels and some fish were now submerged and could be for three weeks depending on the amount of snow coming down from the Welsh mountains. Colin had felt the climate was milder so the melt would be less and therefore last less time. He put away his rod and line and hooks and went out to see if he could be helpful in other ways. The hunters, with whom he shared a hut, were girding themselves up to go into the hills. They wore wool tunics and leather jerkins against the thorns and wrapped skins on their legs so they could run through briars after prey. Their long bows were supple and well used and they carried weighted nets. They carried two poles and twine to tie any carcasses on for the return journey. Colin felt a bit annoyed that most of the catch was given to the chief and his men. They appeared to be providing a protection service but against who? Colin had felt no tension in the village; no one came there or invaded the community, yet the chief sat up in his hall as if plotting world war.

Colin tried to think who came to Britain before the Romans. He knew traders had arrived for centuries coming from the Mediterranean and there was evidence in museums of jewellery and harness dating back long before the Romans came that came from the east. The Phoenicians were supposed to have sailed in the Baltic centuries earlier and even Christ was supposed to have visited Cornwall. He still could not recall any conflicts, but then who would have recorded it? His village were capable of making metal artefacts, jewellery and harness but there were no horses here and only the ox carts which required pretty basic straps and the odd metal rings. The jewellery must be made elsewhere. Arna had a metal pin holding her tunic together, but not of gold and silver. The chief had bronze buckles and pins on his clothes and the fighters had iron weapons. Had they had a history of being invaded hence the need for a fighting force? If anyone wanted to invade they would necessarily come up or across the river but from what he had seen from the Tut the Severn Valley had peaceful settlements like his own; an industrious population uninterested in war or conquest.

All he could remember of history was King Arthur and the endless battles between clans but that was far into the future.

After the hunters set off he made his way down the edge of the flooded Ham to the north of the Swilgate. It swung around the oak grove where the standing stones were and filled all the flat land beyond as well. A rough hewn wooden bridge spanned it to get to the chief's hall but this was almost up to the footpath in water. He wondered what happened if the water rose above the bridge. The chief would be cut off from the village and possibly his food supply. As it was spring all wildlife would be breeding now. He wondered, as in the gaming season, if they held back from killing beasts to allow regeneration of flocks and herds. The hunters had crossed the bridge then set off north to where the forest was thicker. There were many red deer in the forest as well as boar, enough to keep the hall supplied without killing sheep and oxen, even in winter.

He also crossed the bridge and set off along the far side of the Swilgate. In his day this would have been the cricket ground and the allotments and they had built a new council estate there on reasonably flat land. His father had warned they were daft building on the flood plain and whilst the Severn had never risen that far it would only take a particularly severe winter for the snows to build up on Snowdon and send torrents of melt water into the valley. Upton and Evesham had often had serious floods even in recent times. Colin had always been fascinated by the inundation. He recalled his first sight at age four when his father had brought him down Mill Street one evening and the water seemed to be on the verge of coming up into the town. They had sat on the wall in St Mary's lane looking down at the lapping waters, in reality only a few feet deep but to him it looked like the Atlantic Ocean.

Medieval Tewkesbury had adapted to this, building their black and white timbered houses above the high water level on a revetement wall and the Abbey on the high ground. The monks built a water mill on the side of the ham and a mill avon from the great Avon to power it's great wooden wheel. Flour had been ground there since the 11th century. Under the mill was a stone paved cellar that you could enter by a small wooden bridge outside. Colin had been in there lots of times; it was used by various community groups, the WI, Rotarians and the local water painting club but in March it was out of bounds. The water rose up to more than half the walls and somehow drained away before Easter leaving the room dry and airy again for another ten months' use.

The fertile silt that was washed down the river was then deposited on the Hams around Tewkesbury adding to its depth and vitality and allowing rich crops to be grown in summer. The monks had grown wheat and milled it in situ but the Victorians built a massive commercial mill at the other end of the Mill Avon which processed wheat from all over Gloucestershire and Worcestershire and it was sent down to Gloucester docks in massive barges to be exported across the world. All the land round Tewkesbury in Colin's life was arable and the farmers well to do.

He carried on walking bringing him up behind the heath where the sheep grazed at a little height. He could look down on the village and its circular, dun coloured huts and their plumes of blue smoke that looked idyllic. He thought about Sian and her swollen belly, lightly stepping about her duties and he wanted to run back and embrace her. He wished he could know if she thought about him the same way but demonstrations of affection were not evident in their community. People were dignified and respectful if anything.

After he had walked about another mile he could see down to where the bridge crossed the Severn, again it's span only a foot or two above the flood waters, which were swirling dark and brown and carrying rough branches and vegetation. He guessed he was in the area he knew as Twynning, an area of suburbs that housed all the new people arriving to work in the industrial estate in the north of the town. Even in his day the population were changing from a rural farming community to a commercial town, full of newcomers. It was great for the bank. There had only been two banks for all of the sixties but now another bank had come as well as building societies and they had been keeping regular social contacts to encourage more businesses to choose their bank. Colin was not much good at the social side of banking. Vaughan did most of the sucking up to company bosses and loved standing around in bars smoking a cigar. Colin thought he would probably grow into that lifestyle-or not if the present continued.

He walked on northwards; there was a track between hummocks of grass and briar, roughly the A38 continuing along high ground above the Avon on this side. There was very little to see other than the view across the river; forest, scrub and the distant blue hills of Wales, lots of wildfowl by the river and a small herd of deer darting back into the forest at his approach. Eventually he began to feel hungry and set off back to the village thinking about how he would fare if he was on his own. There were no crops at this time of year, no fruit or berries. While he knew the theory of catching game and he did not have the skills; even as a good fisherman with the Ham flooded it was all hopeless for fishing.

In the far distance he could see a row of men scattering seed on one of the upland ploughed fields. He had not seen them ploughing although a wooden plough was stored in the village in winter. It must take them weeks just to do one field he thought. But they needed their oats and barley, straw and fodder for the animals so it was essential the crops flourished. Those three men, he thought, had the future of the whole village in their hands. He watched their rhythmic casting, each in a diagonal to the other, forward for about a quarter mile, then back along the furrows, further beyond his sight. He wondered how they kept the birds off the grain but supposed it was another job for small children.

As he swung along the back of the heath he came upon the chief's men approaching the hall. Some glanced at him and were advised by others that Colin was known to them. Colin pondered just how many were garrisoned here, there seemed to be about twenty and three on horseback and he would have said they were strangers by their demeanour. They were marching up to the hall and he stood and watched as they were challenged and admitted. Clearly friendly but it set him thinking about how many fighting men were in the area should they be invaded. He could remember the story of Boudicca attacking the Romans and decimating Colchester but could not recall any other battles with Britons. He assumed there had been conflict; surely the Britons would not just have let the Romans take over.

Colin decided his stomach could wait no longer and walked back to camp. One elder obviously wanted to know where he had been and why he was empty handed but Colin just smiled and shrugged. It did not stop him getting a share of the hare soup and barley bread.

CHAPTER 8

CRICKLEY HILL

At the setting sun ceremony the new elder -quite a fit looking man who still went out hunting occasionally- spoke to the clan earnestly. Colin sensed the difference in his speech. This was something serious and global. He kept pointing to the south and using both hands to indicate a stepping movement and another fluctuating hand movement that could mean waves of hills. After the tribe had all had their say there seemed to be a general agreement about some plan and some of the people looked at Colin. Whatever the plan involved he gathered it included him although they seemed to think it all very pleasant and positive. Only Sian was upset and she clung to him apparently begging him not to concur but he did not know what was expected of him. He comforted her but against what he did not know. He was looking forward to having a new hut, did he have to get planning permission for it? Who built it? He could see how they were made but needed huge quantities of wood and reeds. Was he just allowed to take these commodities?

How soon could it be achieved? How far pregnant was Sian? Suddenly Colin felt he had all sorts of responsibilities he had not had in his former life. He was to be a father, a partner, a house builder and a provider. He had no parents or brothers to help him out with these massive tasks. How should he start? The following day Mard, at the sun rising ceremony, announced to the tribe that his daughter and Colin were a partnership. There were whoops of joy and pats on the back for him. Everyone seemed very pleased for them both. No doubt births were of paramount importance.

The hut left by the elder who died had been his sole occupancy and the new elder moved in after a purifying ceremony. He was alone having been living with his daughter and her two teenage sons, older daughter and her baby. The three other elders who had died were all living with their own families. Mard and Arna had Sian, her three younger brothers and an older woman whom Colin took to be Arna's mother. He had difficulty guessing ages. Arna's mother had grey hair but could have been forty five. That would make Arna about thirty and Sian about fifteen at the most. He believed their lifespan was much shorter than modern man and assumed the elders were in their fifties. There were fewer men than women anyway and to find a single man in his fifties was quite rare. Several of the village women were pregnant. The ceremony in October was no doubt responsible and it would mean they were now five months pregnant and would give birth in July. He wondered when Sian was due. She did not look four months pregnant. His birthday was in September, maybe it would be then?

Colin was welcomed more often into Mard's home for meals and company than before. Although he slept with his three room mates, he still only returned there at night after sitting around the charcoal brazier listening to the family's chatter and trying to learn more about the language. Sian almost waited on him which made him feel embarrassed, although he guessed she did it to impress her parents more than him. She was always offering an extra pillow to lay on or bits of extra food when they had any. Due to the lack of salt or sugar there were no preservatives but they made a sort of weak cider out of crab apples that had thick froth on top and which they drank hot and they had a hoard of unshelled hazelnuts as well. By the end of March Colin was fishing daily and producing at least one large fish for the pot. Eels were plentiful as were fresh water oysters. The villagers had a type of pig which all seemed to be pregnant which would produce a good supply of food and could live on acorns in the forest to fatten them up for winter. There were plentiful supplies of wildfowl in the water meadows if the villagers could catch them. They had no specific method of hunting them and used a type of bolas for geese and ducks and the archers were able at hitting a swan or two.

Miraculously, the supply of turnips, apples and roots lasted just until the winter ended and prevented starvation before the spring brought greens and wild garlic and while the sheep were suckling the production of cheese went down, but there were hardened cheeses left over from winter and the grains held out to make bread and oatcakes. Despite his added muscles from the bellows and his shaven head, Colin began to feel considerably thinner and less healthy as the winter ended and no doubt was suffering from vitamin deficiency. He knew certain foods had what he required such as carrots having vitamin A but there were no carrots, no citrus fruits or supplements like his mother had given him. He worried that his hair or teeth would fall out and he get some disease like rickets as his body had not been used to this deprivation like the village people. Shortly after Sian's family announced their partnership some of the elders were clearly planning some task for Colin. Firstly they asked him to teach the younger boys about salmon fishing and eel netting. After two weeks of this they took him off into the forest where they selected some straight tall birch trees, choosing six. Each of them had the task of cutting down a tree with a hand axe with a metal edge, removing the branches and cutting the poles to about fifteen feet. Colin thought this was how they started building a round house. It appeared to have a series of vertical posts let into the ground with a lintel all round to support the roof. It was let into a shallow circular hole so that the soil was packed around it up to about three feet to the eaves. More poles of a thinner radius were tied in to make the roof spars with a circular wreath of hazel twigs holding the hole open at the top. Hazel and wattle and mud and hair daub was then used to make the walls. The floor was beaten earth with a central hearth stone for the brazier to sit on. No windows but a low door was built in with a frame of skins pulled across at night or in bad weather. The roofs were thatched with reeds from the river, pinned down with twine and stones.

However they seemed more interested in how many poles Colin could carry. They were four inches in diameter and quite heavy but they seemed keen to load him with four poles. His slighter colleagues carried two each and they brought the branches back for kindling. By the time they got back to camp Colin was in some pain and bruised from the poles shifting about on his shoulders and he could not see why they could not all share the weight. That night before the setting sun ritual the elders took him to one side and tried to explain their plans. They made a map in the soil and pointed to Bredon Hill and Prestbury Hill and the far Malverns. They drew in the mud of the ground and he could recognise the river Severn snaking south and some of the local terrain. They then drew a straight line between them from hill to hill and used their fingers to indicate walking along the marks. Presumably they wanted to go on a long walk over the hills. Colin wondered if they wanted him to tell them what the landscape was like south of there or if they thought he came from that area. Colin nodded but still did not understand what they were proposing and could not see what these plans had to do with building his hut.

The next day after sun rise ceremony the new elder made an announcement to the clan who all looked at Colin with admiration. He pointed South and to the poles laid out tidily and roped together in threes then called out three other men. Of these two were elders; wiry brown men in their forties and the other a youth who was probably the largest of the clan who looked quite fed up by the choice. The elder waved his arm towards the south east and was firing up the tribe to some plan he had in mind. There was some dissent and apprehension in the crowd and questions asked. Obviously this was a plan the previous leader had not supported but the new elder was keen to get on with and somehow Colin's size or knowledge was intrinsic to the plan. Well he did have a good knowledge of the countryside but where he knew of towns and roads there would be none. The direction he pointed out would take them to Cheltenham and over the hills to Cirencester. He supposed that even then there must have been some sort of settlement in those river valleys.

After the speech and a general agreement to continue Sian was tearful and clung to him and Colin realised he was meant to go away with these men over the hills but the way she was carrying on suggested he was being asked to do something dangerous or leaving for good. He tried to comfort her as best he could but thought if they planned to be fighting or hunting he was the last person they would have chosen.

His bark calendar showed him it was about March 31st and the villagers were preparing for another ceremony. This time the women were the ones who were adorned not in mud and furs but with fine boughs with new leaves and catkins. The procession again took place in the stone circle with the women dancing and singing at dawn and the priest incanting over them. Many of the women were pregnant and Sian was joining in but her sad face turned to Colin often which indicated to him far more than the men's explanations what his fate may be.

The next day before dawn Colin was woken by the youth from the previous day's discussion. He pointed to all of Colin's possessions; his leather belt, wool sweater, hat, wool rags, pattens, knife, razor as well as his sheep skins on the bed and motioned to him to bring them. He wound his arms in a revolving motion and showed Colin a bag like skin of his own possessions. On his leather belt was his bow, quiver and arrows, a spear and some snares for hares. He had a net in his bag and some bronze knives, bone slivers and flint stones for cutting or skinning. Colin wrapped his two skins together with some twine, his possessions inside some rags. He still had his trousers with pockets in which he kept his pocket knife and razor.

On leaving his hut he went straight to Sian's hut to say goodbye. It was clear the other men had a planned journey on which he was to take part but he could only gauge that it would be for some time by Sian's reaction to the news. She was all over him, weeping and hugging him and he did not even know where he was going. Surely she would not take on so if it was only a few days? She must be expecting him to be gone for ever or at least a few weeks to be so distraught. He thought of his child growing inside her and wished he could be with her during the pregnancy not off on some journey.

Sian gave him a sling of linen with food for the journey. There were barley grains, dried pork, some oat rusks and a little salt and gave him a final hug before they set off on the road south. They passed the chief's hall and the guards gave them a wave and wished them well. Everyone seemed to know where they were going except him. Through the woods they collected the six long poles they had cut the day before. They had been de-barked and trimmed and pointed at one end. Colin and the youth had four poles on twine loops from their shoulders so had to walk in line, the elders had one pole on each side but Colin noticed they carried substantial packs with food and axes, bows and spears, and each had a metal pot on a string hanging from their poles. They set off at a brisk pace and Colin found he had to shift the weight of the twine loops to prevent the twine cutting in to his shoulders. The men chattered among themselves and Colin felt bored and hard done by. He was anxious they again would be asking him to do something that was beyond him, that he was being used in some inappropriate way, that they were taking advantage of him now he had got a child by Sian and he began to feel the old depression creeping back and weighing him down.

For miles all he could see was forest. All the valley of the Severn outside the flood plain was thick with oak and birch and where the A38 would one day be was dense with trees. The vale of Evesham stretched behind in an uninterrupted sea of bright green as far as he could see; only the tops of the hills stood proud and bare in this wild landscape and beyond the river the Welsh Hills rose grey and cold. On the highest point of the ground beyond the village they looked back to Bredon Hill where stood a single sentinel post. Colin had not noticed a post there from the village viewpoint but assumed they were now viewing it from a different angle. They looked south to another raised area, probably Leckhampton Hill and he could see at the edge of his vision slight mounds and irregularities on it's crown.

After three hours they had reached the bottom of what he knew to be Cleeve Hill. They set down their poles in a birch copse as it was thinning out towards the escarpment. Colin eyed the 30% slope with trepidation. It was one thing as a schoolboy climbing the steep and crumbling face of the hill with your mates with nothing to carry but humping six fifteen foot poles which were creating a deformity on his shoulders was another matter. He wondered if it would be easier making two trips using the elder's slings twice over. They squatted by a tiny stream that came out of the foot of the hill and drank crystal clear water. No chemicals, fertilizers or pollutants in this he thought. They built a small fire using a stick and a flint and some dried grass to catch the light and after a while had a good hot blaze going.

The youth, Yarren, went off with his bow and arrows and by the time the fire was hot he came back with two pigeons. Colin helped to pluck and gut the birds which went into the pot Eiran had brought, some dry herbs and barley and they made the best of it with some rusks from their packs. It was not satisfying but they needed the rest. Colin rubbed his shoulders without achieving any respite from the pain and his feet were aching from walking so far in wood pattens strapped to them. Oh for a pair of walking boots and thick socks he thought.

After about two hours they agreed to make the ascent up the slope and reluctantly doused the fire and hauled their packs round their bodies and looked woefully at their poles. Colin being the tallest went in the rear so the slope would not be so acute and he padded his shoulders with his sweater and set off. He found the men had a steady pace which was easy to climb and they went across the slope, turned and went back, rather than trying to scale it in one. Slowly they rose above the valley and Colin was able to view the space that would one day be Cheltenham.

Below he could see the denser line of trees following the river Chelt though the valley. It started near to Cleeve Hill and wound it's way through what would be Charlton Kings and he traced the line across Cox's meadow. Just where it flattened out he could see a clearing with more huts and some cultivated fields and a spire of smoke rising through the treetops. The Town Hall would one day rise out of this space, previously untouched by buildings before the Georgians decided a spa would be a great little money spinner. They had some difficulty finding one and even then moved its position to make it more accessible to tourists. But now just a valley full of mature trees sloping gently towards the Severn in the distance.

Both elders moved back and forth across the top of the hill, looking north and south and eventually one ushered Colin forward and pointed to a depression of wet soil. Colin had put down the poles on the ground but the elder, called Eiran, pulled out a metal headed horn mattock and indicated that Colin should dig a hole and plant the pole there.

Suddenly it dawned on Colin what they were doing. They were erecting poles on the visible summits of the hills, similar to the line of warning beacons across the South Downs during the Spanish Armada, he recalled. He set about digging as neat a hole as possible. After about ten minutes he had gone quite deep. The ground was wet after the winter and although the soil was thin on the sandstone of the hill he found they had chosen a depression where there was about two feet of soil, giving it the best chance of sinking. Once they got to the bedrock they indicated he should keep chipping at the stone to make more of a hole. Although he had gained strength and muscle from his active lifestyle the winter hunger had not given him much energy reserves. He could see how the tribesmen became so wiry and tough. Some winters must be harder than the one he experienced and their energy levels drop dangerously low. He had no fat reserves left on his body to cope with any extra demands such as digging holes in the rock. Nevertheless he managed to cut about a foot into the rock before the elders produced some iron headed tool that sort of gouged out a round hole for the post. It took about an hour before they were able to turn the first pole into the slot. While he was digging they had been scouting around for some smaller stones. An area where the soil had eroded exposed a bit of cliff where the rock was fractured and they brought rocks to wedge the pole into the hole that was almost a metre deep. As they stood back and looked up the twelve foot left exposed they, as one, let out a little cheer of triumph. How little people change, thought Colin.

After their achievement they sat down and drank a little water they had collected at the spring. His exertions made him feel cheerful, especially now he had some idea what they were going to do. He wondered if this was a local plan or a national task they were joining in with. As they sat, the elders pointed back towards Bredon Hill where the post Colin had seen the previous week was a small erect feature on a bald upland down. He thought that maybe they had only recently erected that one since receiving some information from afar. He wished he had paid more attention at school when they had studied how the roads were originally built in England.

After they had relaxed it was about teatime but there was no indication they were going to eat. Colin had two oat rusks left over and ate one with a piece of dried pork as he walked alone. They now had five poles to carry but he and Yarren still had four between them. He was getting used to the weight but negotiating the ridges and slopes of the hill made the constant shifting painful. He did not relish the afternoon as he did not know how far they were going to walk. He assumed they would be heading to Crickley Hill but they did not go down into the valley but kept walking south east along the top of the hill. Colin could see why they brought poles. There were no trees on the tops of hills but the woods in the valley were tangled masses of undergrowth and small trees and none that were suitable as the coppiced birches had been.

The sky seemed huge from the top of the hills and Colin breathed in the uncontaminated air. No pollution here, he thought, and everything we eat or drink is pure. It struck him how damaged the world was since man had come and settled in England after the ice age. Even the wood fires were causing carbon and ash to be sent into the air. He could understand how sitting round the camp fire could become unhealthy and why the families used charcoal in their huts. A cool wind sprung up and the effort of digging the hole had made his clothes feel damp and despite walking he began to feel chilled. The others chatted away as they walked but he was excluded by his ignorance. He made a mental note to try harder to learn their language when he got back instead of trading the names of body parts with Sian.

About an hour's walk later they started to go up hill again to a peak he did not recognise. He felt rather than noticed that they must be walking towards Cirencester but Crickley Hill, now behind them, was out of sghte from this angle. They walked on steadily climbing a ridge which gave them a brilliant view over the Colne Valley, its steep sides and rushing water seemed wilder than the pleasant, meandering Severn Valley. It was not evident how they could get down to the water although Colin felt really thirsty, and they had consumed all their water they had collected at the spring.

Eventually Eiran stopped and put down his pole. He and Yarren looked back towards Cleeve Hill and forward southwards. Now Colin could see that they had come round to a point that was between Crickley Hill and Cleeve Hill and Bredon was in the far distance, too far off to see the pole though. The two men walked about trying to work out a line between the three poles. They got Colin and Yarren to stand about fifty feet either side and lined them up with the pole on Cleeve Hill and the camp fires at Crickley Hill. This upland was much better covered in soil and Colin thought he would have an easier job digging a metre deep hole. They selected a place and indicated Colin should start digging. With his metal edged pick it was easy and Yarren used his hands to pull the loose soil out of the hole. However it was too large for the pole and after half an hour Yarren, Dai and Eiran came back with two largish rocks to jam the pole in.

Colin had sat down while he waited. The hill was so different from the one he knew. In his time it was grazed by sheep for two centuries and had short wiry turf. Now it was long and full of teasels and weeds. The butterflies looked much the same only there were many of them and birds were evident everywhere especially of the crow variety. He watched some finches foraging for seeds in the hummocky grass and lay back to watch the clouds scudding by. He thought about time and how it affected everything, three billion years ago it might have been Jurassic, the Cotswolds not even built, England under a warm sea full of shellfish ready to build the limestones and chalks that one day would become English scenery.

As he dug deeper the soil became stony then turned to shale like rock. He tried to make the hole narrower to hold the pole upright but it was still a difficult job at three feet down. He felt they really needed proper tools such as an auger and there was no reason they could not forge one. The word auger is a Roman word he thought so presumably they existed around that time, just not available in his village.

Eventually the pole was erected, eleven feet proud of the soil and packed in with rocks, stone and mud. This time there was no cheering. All of them were tired and hungry and the wind was whipping up a dampness that chilled them even when working. The waning sun was quite warm on their faces as they turned towards Crickley Hill. The terrain here was more abrupt, cliffs of sandstone falling into a ravine between the two hills. Dai and Eiran were talking together and a sense of urgency was apparent as they packed their gear, did not sit down and left Colin and Yarren to put the four poles back in their slings and turned south towards the valley.

Colin knew the way between the two hills well. He had often gone on expeditions to Crickley Hill prehistoric hill fort as a teenager and knew there was a route due south from the top of Leckhampton Hill. However one of the elders, Dai, indicated that he must stay behind by the pole. Colin and the other two set off with the four poles heavily on their shoulders and edged their way down the escarpment into a hung valley. The route was covered in trees and it was difficult to manoeuvre the poles. Then they made their way across a stream to start climbing the further slope. After about an hour they came across a clearing with a guard post; or that was how Colin interpreted it. Three men, heavily armed, stood watching their ascent towards the hill but made no move. As they approached Colin's party stopped, put down their poles and Eiran went forward and spoke. He was gesticulating and speaking about the hills waving his arms upward and around the valley. It was clear that they understood quickly the purpose of the party's approach and ushered them on their way, a young scout going ahead, and they shouldered their poles reluctantly.

On climbing a steep slope where they had no view of the hill fort they suddenly rounded an outcrop and viewed from below a bare mountain of soil and turf. Somehow it looked unassailable from where they were standing. There was no one in sight and a worn broad path went around the hill leading to a wooden palisade and gateway. As they climbed they could look back to the dells and vales behind where there were cattle grazing shepherded by small boys.

This was an altogether larger enterprise than his village without its rampart or palisade or even a fence other than the sheep corral. More men were opening the gate, prompted by the scout before them and before entering they waited for another elder to be brought to the gateway. Colin had a chance to look at the construction of the fort close to. There were two gateways, one behind the other, with a walkway behind the first where men could be lookouts. The gateway was square, butted up against the palisade which was about twelve foot high and made of straight posts similar to those he carried. He began to muse on the amount of labour that would be needed to erect such a fence. It had taken an hour for him to dig one hole. Here the palisade marched away round the hill a veritable forest of trees required to build it and an army of men to fell and trim the trees, carry them to the site, as there were few big trees on the hill. Each post was lashed into the one next door with twine and inside horizontal poles to strengthen the whole. Outside, except where the gate was, they had excavated a deep ditch, thirty feet across, and in the bottom were placed short pointed posts that looked lethal if one were to fall into the ditch. As the hill grew steeper the ditch ended and the steepness of the hill became its defence.

After some greetings they were invited in and were shown to the chief's long house, similar to the one Colin saw in

Tewkesbury camp. There was a lot of talking and some of the frothy cider was produced along with barley cakes. Colin tried to pick up from their speech some clues as to what the plan was. Clearly the chief knew that they were coming and he stared curiously at Colin while his strange appearance was explained. Eventually they went out with their poles to the highest point of the hill within the camp. Everywhere there was business going on. On one side Colin recognised a smelting yard with covered in ovens and heaps of raw ores. There were carts, sturdy and new looking and a wheelwright was fixing a broken spoke of one of them. The incessant hammering of smiths and wrights went on and beyond, in the distance he could see the round huts and women sitting outside with their looms and the occasional plume of smoke and whiff of cooking.

Eiran and Yarren set about looking north to where Dai had been left by the pole on the Hill. In the distance they could just see his small figure standing by the pole. Suddenly a flag sprung up, yellow and clear from his position and Eiran similarly produced a yellow cloth with which he took a stick and wound the cloth roughly to make a flag. They stood and watched as the two men copied each other's movements to acknowledge they could see each other. Then Eiran directed Yarren to take one of the poles and stand it on the high point. Colin was ordered to go behind with his pole and wait instructions. They were now standing about eight feet apart, with a pole each while Eiran and Dai communicated with the flag where this pole should stand. Colin assumed Dai could see some distant headland with which they were to line up the poles and Yarren moved back and forth until Dai's flag suddenly dropped from sight. This was the position to place the pole. As he went to get the mattock Yarren signalled Colin to hold both poles in line one in each hand. He could now see why he was chosen for this task; as the tallest and with the longest arms he was ideal for lining up the posts as far apart as possible, getting the most accurate positioning.

As he stood still, his back to the westering sun, a pole in each hand, he was casting a long shadow across the turf of the hill and suddenly he recognised the shadow as a picture he already knew. A tall man, arms apart, with a pole in each, silhouetted against the hillside. Where had he seen that before? Then it hit him. It had been in the National Geographic in the bank's foyer. A picture just like that cut out on chalk on a hillside somewhere in Sussex- The Long Man of Wilmington. And here he was; the long man. Helping to build a new Britain.

CHAPTER 9

THE ROAD

The elder had determined the hole was to be dug here. They pointed and their own men brought picks of deer antler and began digging a hole in the chalk for the new pole. Colin hoped this meant he could stop carrying two poles too. By sunset they had finished their task and the pole stood proud and linked up with the pole on Cleeve Hill, on Bredon Hill and so on back into the Severn Valley and Wales. Colin began to feel a sense of achievement.

They stayed the night in the village. It was much busier and there were several fire hearths burning. They also had music played on lyre like instruments, more sophisticated than the whistle and drum at Tewkesbury. At length they were invited to join a group of men who were seated round a good fire and offered meat and barley cakes. There was lamb and rabbit, a positive feast compared to his own village but he supposed they had less fish because there was no great river here, just a small stream in the valley. To think that a ten mile walk made such a different life for people. Theirs was a camp for defence. Even an army would have trouble approaching up here, the ditch and double gate would only be assailed by fire perhaps and there was little water to deal with that. But it gave a sense of absolute security compared with the open waterside dwellings with which he was familiar. Who would they fear he wondered? The Welsh were only a few miles away from Tewkesbury but there was no sign of hostility. Perhaps these people were the Welsh, occupying England before they were driven out by the Romans.

As they sat and gnawed bones and drank cider the atmosphere grew jolly and a man came and sang songs that were clearly narrative. They smiled and nodded as he sang. Perhaps an old favourite. As he sang Colin had the distinct feeling he could hear bag pipes. The plaintive whine was unmistakable. He started to look past the fire into the darkness beyond, where seven or eight other fires flamed. He felt it would be offensive to walk away while the man was singing but he wanted to see the instrument being played away beyond the glow of the hearth.

After a while the song ended, people cheered and Colin made to get up. He staggered a little-the cider was strong-but made his way to another site where a troupe of girls were dancing and, yes, a young man was playing a small version of the bagpipes. It had an irresistible sound, almost like a hurdy gurdy, that made him want to get up and dance too, but he sat still and let the melody transport him into the magical pagan world of gods and visions and strange beliefs.

He did not recall going to bed but woke up next morning on a pile of sheepskins in a shared hut.

His fellows had brought with them some bronze knives and brooches and were bartering for food. They were given dried pork strips, apples, barley cakes and salt as well as some dried fruit that looked like plums. They also gave them leather slings so that Colin and the other youth could carry poles at their waists rather than their shoulders but it did not relieve Colin's bruises that day. By sunrise they were on their way again, taking the steep path back to the ravine and making their way along the valley bottom until they came out on the open hill opposite, which Colin knew as Birdlip. This time they made their way along a ridgeway that must have been the main route to Crickley Hill from the south. They walked for about three hours towards what Colin thought would be Cirencester, the A217. The views west were to the welsh hills and far distant forests in the Severn Vale. He could see why they lived on hill tops. Most of the countryside was dense forest, no paths or clearings just bramble, bracken and undergrowth between great oaks and elms and hornbeams. Colin missed the variety of trees he knew. There were no chestnuts or beeches. They would have to wait for the Romans to bring them.

They stood above the area where modern Cirencester would be two thousand years later. He could see a gentle vale with smoke rising from morning fires and what looked like another palisade. They looked back to where Crickley hill was a distant crest in the north and saw the slight slender post atop the highest point. Somewhere beyond was the place he now thought of as home, his wife and her family. The familiar smell of treated sheepskins and wet wool, of baking and stews, of lying in bed with Sian with her wrapped in his arms, safe and warm. He wondered what she was doing without him. She was carrying his child but he knew nothing of their moral codes, if they had them. If your partner was away did they have a sense of loyalty or faithfulness or would Sian start a relationship with someone else. He had no idea where they were going or how long they would be away. Sian was four or five months pregnant.

Had he been just used to get her with a large child and jettisoned or did they respect his right to her and the child? Never in his life had he felt so adrift and anxious. He realised how much a civilised society took for granted the laws and behaviours that were a given. These people seemed to live by similar rules. There was no violence that he could see, everyone had to work according to their ability and strength; individual abilities were cherished and cultivated whether you were a labourer, cook or singer. They had never heard of Christianity but their morals appeared to be the same. He hoped that Sian was staying faithful to him and that he would get back to see her as soon as their task was over.

They descended the Cotswold hills to the gentle valley of the Colne at Cirencester and from a distance Colin could see the plumes of smoke rising from the larger settlement. As they approached it was far more of a town than Crickley Hill. There were still groups of round huts and a wooden hall but there was also a wooden stockade around a central core of buildings with several long huts built up on stilts which looked like storage barns. In Tewkesbury they kept the fodder and grain in round huts and the children and dogs spent their days chasing away rats and mice to preserve the crop. Here there were wooden piles with space below so that any vermin could be seen approaching and dispatched.

As they approached he began to focus on the men at the gate and was taken aback to see they were in armour, Roman armour. The two guards at the first gatehouse were in brown cloth with metal plated kilts and carrying spears. Colin assumed that this was for show as he could see no risk of attack but as they approached the Romans were alert and ready for any eventuality. Colin stared and stared. They started to peruse him and wanted to see his pack. Eiran was talking to them in a way they seemed to understand although he did not recognise it as Latin. Eiran was explaining about Colin who stood out like a sore thumb. They hailed a passing man and asked him to go and find someone within, making them all wait outside the gate. Eiran and he stood peaceably aside. Colin imagined what it would be like in Tewkesbury in his day if their entry was questioned; harsh words, a scuffle or a fight. Maybe these peoples had more sophistication than in his day.

Soon a native came with two Roman soldiers and the guard were instructed to let them pass. He was watched silently by the guard but once past the gate was greeted by some townsfolk as if expected and after a meal of roast hare, gruel and greens Colin made indication he wanted to go to the river to bathe. After two days of digging, marching and carrying the heavy poles he had been alternately sweating and shivering and felt filthy. His companions did not seem to worry about being unclean and while he had seen them bathing in the river in summer they seemed content to stink all winter. He remembered the river at Cirencester as a child, a pleasant greensward ran alongside where people walked dogs and sat and picnicked on the banks. Now it was grey with winter mud but he managed to find a quiet spot and plunged in the gravelly shallows until the cold drove him out again. He used his sheepskin wraps to wipe off the wet and then climbed back into his linen shirt that Sian had made for him, his trousers and pullover.

When he went back to his friends they were sitting around the communal fire talking to some elders. Colin got the impression they were informing his companions about the countryside beyond. They were talking numbers on their hands, possibly distances to the next trig point. Colin wondered what happened when they had used all their poles. They would then be about 30 miles from Tewkesbury if they kept up this pattern. How far would they get? Where were they going? Colin initially thought they might go down the Severn valley to the estuary and hit some port like Gloucester or Bristol but they had been heading inland away from the Severn valley so presumably had a destination in mind.

They stayed in the camp for another day. Colin was fascinated the way the Romans dealt with the locals. Their behaviour was clearly different; they kept to their own lodgings in wooden huts and did not socialise with the locals. But they did not interfere either. Colin saw them communicate with the local residents in the same language so they must have had a lengthy period of communication with them to be so familiar. When he listened to the Romans communicating between themselves it certainly did not sound like Latin at all. He could remember quite a lot of Latin from school but none of it seemed familiar to his ear. Maybe as they moved across Europe their language changed to fit the locality. If so he could assume they had been around this area for at least a generation which put the date about 50 AD.

Watching the people around him he began to think that travelling was a better option than staying in the village. There was so much going on everywhere. Building huts, carpenters working wood, a whole camp of jewellery makers polishing stones and pummelling metal into beautiful artefacts. He noticed the locals were listening to instructions from the Romans building an edifice over the Water and came to the conclusion this was the baths or latrine for the soldiers.

Everyone seemed a bit wary of Colin here, being so much taller and stronger than anyone else. The Romans were also quite short though muscular and well exercised. His companions reassured people he was harmless and trustworthy as they went about and he began to feel a bit like a giant from legend. One of the girls in the jeweller's camp took a liking to him and showed him how they dredged the gravel looking for pieces of quartz and pebble to use for decorative stones. They were polished with some sort of stone paste on chamois leather in a job for dextrous fingers.

Further along he found a potters camp, turning out round lipped pots with basic decorations incised on the body of the clay. There were numerous kilns built around in stone and fired with charcoal and bellows like those they used in the smelting yards at Tewkesbury. The pots were fired decorated, fired again and cooled then loaded on to carts then taken away south along a dirt track that was surprisingly wide.

Chapter 10

Romani

Colin and the elders walked across the last stretch of scrub towards a causeway standing proud of the landscape. From the south it formed a straight parameter or raised highway flanked by deep ditches on both sides. As they approached they watched a team of soldiers digging with short blunt spades and throwing soil and rocks onto the central core about twelve feet across. Two deep ditches were being scored to produce rubble for the roadway. Alongside drew up carts carrying sand and limestone slabs. Before their eyes the road was being manufactured across the lowlands of Gloucestershire from Cirencester. The guard, presumably a centurion, turned to watch their approach. Even with his helmet he was not as tall as Colin and he gave him a sour look. He spoke his own language, not the local tongue and barked out something to them, pointing at the work site. One of the diggers, a Briton, looked sideways without stopping work. "He wants to know your business", he seemed to be saying. Eiran signalled that all of the four of them wanted to join in the work party. Colin was confused. Why should they offer to work when the Romans were doing such a good job? Did they want to be enslaved and worked to a pulp? Colin's memory of history lessons were that Romans enslaved people and forced them to work; starved them and killed them if they ran off. He seemed to recall they were known to be cruel to people who were not Roman and pretty immoral as well.

Between their interpreter and the Centurion they made it clear they wanted to work and he grasped their intention. He looked them up and down and then pointed at Colin and said something significant. Colin was taken aback. Were his friends going to sell him into slavery? Was this the purpose of their long trek? The interpreter grinned. "You three can dig. He can work in the quarry". Colin had no way of knowing what was being said, that his skills were being bartered, but felt unable to protest. Soon the others were being hussled to the front edge of the ditches and given spades. Two other workers gave them up to take a break. Colin was directed towards the ox-cart some way back where they were unloading rough cut small slabs of limestone and was shown where to load the stones so the mason could fit them into the complex diamond shape layout, with its gentle camber to either side. The road building was done methodically. After the ditches were dug on each side, exactly the same width apart, the soil thrown up to build the causeway was being smoothed and pummelled in with a metal ram. Layers of rock and soil were built up to the last camber which was covered in a layer of sand about four inches thick. That in turn was covered with a layer of limestone slabs about two feet square set into the surface, a bit like crazy paving, and the edges lined with kerb stones. The surface was smooth and curved like any modern road and at the last a layer of sand was shovelled on top. Colin was commandeered to help shift the slabs up to the mount where two masons fitted them expertly into the close bound surface. As he worked, Colin looked back down the length of the new road; as far as he could see the creamy criss-cross paving disappeared over the horizon.

Once the wagon was unloaded he was told to get on it and the oxen were turned round and driven back along the road towards the lower slopes of the Cotswolds. Other carts loaded with stone passed them going back and Colin noticed how different the workers looked. Some swarthy and dark skinned with their hair covered in coloured cloths, reminded him of Sikhs, others were clearly Britons, more were Roman soldiers. After about half an hour the cart turned to the left across some scrubland and through the trees along a worn track that came out in a great scar in the hillside, a quarry. Colin was amazed how much of the hillside was being dug away so quickly. Mainly Britons were at work with iron headed picks and chisels, splitting the stone and uncovering more layers of the glistening rocks. The air was full of dust and noise and he decided he had got the worse option compared to Eiran and the others who at least were out in the countryside. The workers were cutting back and exposing the stratified stone, levering apart the layers and breaking off slabs about two feet across. Where there was debris other workers were loading carts for hardcore and the good slabs were loaded into the cart Colin had travelled on. Even young boys were engaged in this task. Colin set to work but wondered what the purpose was of offering himself up for this. Were they slaves? If so why did Eiran and Yarren walk straight into it so willingly?

After the cart was loaded he and another Briton walked the cart back to the road and up a ramp on to the new road surface, along with a rubble cart before them. Colin was glad to be walking not lifting the slabs of stone. His hands were sore and he wished he had gloves of some sort, but the others did not have them. He wondered if anyone had invented gloves yet. Perhaps he could make a killing as a glove maker in his new world. It was quite pleasant strolling along, above the land at the slow pace of the oxen, able to look about himself and the landscape.

By the time they returned another section of the road was ready for paving and the section ahead ready for hardcore. Colin was intrigued with the smooth running of the project. No one got in each other's way; each party had a period of rest while they awaited the next supply to arrive and each person seemed suited to the task. The skilled Romans worked without orders and the Britons were ordered what to do but not harried or abused. The diggers worked in threes, two on, one at rest and every half hour the centurions ordered them to change round. There was a water cart with a cistern which those at rest could get a cup of water in a ladle and the Romans had supplies with them of wine and food.

After he had loaded three carts the dusk was beginning to draw in. At this time of year it would be about 7pm or later. The centurion called a halt. Tools were put into the carts, the Romans lined up behind their centurion and started to march back down the road they had just built and willingly behind, tramped the weary Britons.

Colin looked at Eiran and shrugged his shoulders and raised his eyebrows in query. He did not know if such gestures were inherent but Eiran smiled and pointed him to follow the troop. He urged Colin forward and fell in behind. The Romans kept up a fast pace but it was easy to follow as the surface of the new road was smooth and soft with sand. After about an hour's march and already the sun setting they approached a solid silhouette against the darkening sky. Colin could make out a tall stockade with some sort of manned watch tower in the front wall. There were flaming torches from inside and fires were lit outside. Colin watched the Romans file into the fort while the Britons sloped aside to where the fires were lit on the outside.

There were at least thirty men sitting around three or four fires, their backs to the stockade wall and in places rough frames with skins that were strung like tents had been erected as shelters. The stars were coming out but it was not a cold night and the camp felt jolly and bright. As soon as they returned some of the Britons came out of the fort bearing trays and baskets. On them were a variety of things Colin had not seen for a year and some he had never seen. There were dates and olives, flat breads, meat patties that smelled like faggots, dried fish and oysters. It was like a mirage in that desolate landscape, as if Colin had been transported to the Mediterranean. The men ate like dogs, scooping up food with their hands and wiping the trays with the breads.

Clearly working for the Romans had its benefits. Water was brought out in pottery flagons and he and Yarren filled their skins for later. Eating the salt fish would make them thirsty. Into the night they bedded down as best they could and Colin wrapped himself in his sheepskins. He listened to the raucous noise from inside the fort getting louder and louder and he realised they were the Romans getting drunk. At last they fell into an exhausted slumber and Colin dreamed of Sian and of comfort and ecstasy.

The next morning they were woken at dawn by a trumpet call. His companions briefly saluted the rising sun and tucked into saffron coloured buns and more water. Soon they were off back down the road, Colin turning off with the ox cart to the quarry to start the day's work. The other workers had skins of water and the dusty air made Colin choke with a parched throat. He indicated to his companion and was relieved that he offered him some of his water. He was surprised how altruistic people were. Presumably there was plenty of water so sharing was not a particular favour. Maybe in drought or famine people would not be so helpful. He had spent so long living off the land he had never been in need of basics but certainly he had missed variety and choice. Here there was an atmosphere of plenty; fruits and meat and fish a plenty and apparently the food was part of the pay for work. Yarren had taken a skin for water all day but it was only enough for one man and he wondered how he could obtain a skin bag for himself. He had no items to barter other than his pen knife and he was not willing to give that up lightly. After about four hours Colin reckoned about 11 am a cart came up the road and to his relief it carried food and water. True it was only bread, dried fruit and water and some strange dark paste. Some put it on their bread, others just ate it dry. Colin thought it seemed familiar; a sweet sour taste that he quite liked. After about half an hour they were back on their feet lugging limestone paving off the cart and on to the raised road. Goodness, what he would do for a mug of strong tea.

At the end of the second day Colin tried to talk to Eiran, Dai and Yarren about what they were doing here. He used his fingers to try to indicate how long they would be doing this work; he hoped it was not going to be a permanent job. Eiran could see what he was asking and waved his hands down to say "calm down, it will be ok". He raised his arms toward the sun and drew them over his head like sun rise and sunset and put his head on one side. Colin put up one finger for one day and Eiran held his hands up three times - thirty days. Colin felt a little reassured. For some reason they would work for a month and that would be about the end of May. What did that signify?

Each day they made about two hundred yards of road and got further and further away from the stockade. When they had started it was about three miles back now nearer six and they were beginning to bring up wood to build another stockade. He wished he had listened in history classes now. He knew Hadrian's Wall had military camps all along it and he believed that roads had posts along them at mile intervals and forts at ten miles. He wondered about the quarry; it was further and further away from the work site each day. Perhaps it was the best source of the stone they wanted?

While he had no sense of oppression it was impossible to slacken without the Romans getting quite stern. No one threatened him or showed him the whip or rod but all the workers kept up a rhythm and pace that if he stopped for a few moments he broke their stride so all of them chivvied each other along, only the centurion keeping an eye on the time. He did this by means of a sand clock mounted on a wagon. It took an hour for the sand to run down out of a crock into a bowl. The two men were moved round to give the third a break and the crock was filled with sand again. Hour by hour they toiled and ten times the crock was refilled until the sun westered and they amassed their tools.

After a few days Colin was also commandeered to help build the new stockade. Wood felled was being brought to the site and with some very competent military carpenters, a watch tower was constructed with a broad stair up the rear. After they had measured the pieces it all fitted together and Colin realised they had a template they were working to. He recalled the Romans built bridges and siege engines the same way and he admired their perseverance and single mindedness. There was no decision making. Each watch tower, stockade, latrine and gateway was identical to the thousands they had built before, all the way from Rome through France and southern Britain to Cirencester. The bare resources changed. Here the road was limestone, but he guessed it was different stone according to the local geology. The wood would be different along the way but each fort was the same, each guard post the identical form of the one before.

The first three days had been hell. Colin had never done labouring work before except gardening and his muscles ached all over. He slept like a log and when the trumpet sounded he could hardly move at first. After a week he started to notice the muscles building in different places. His torso had marked ridges across his abdomen from bending and lifting slabs and his back muscles were beginning to bulge so that when he put his arms down they stopped them touching his rib cage. He felt quite proud of his physique. The Romans were also muscular but small and wiry and next to them Colin looked like a God. When they disappeared into the fort at night he assumed they already had a bath house; they looked tidy and clean, cut their hair and shaved their faces. They also smelt of herbs and scent. Compared to the Britons who barely washed off the mud in a small stream and stank of all bodily excretions the Romans were scented and oiled. They were viewed by the Britons with suspicion and mockery but Colin was impressed. He wished he could go into the fort and see what they were up to inside.

When he was working he was alongside the other Britons mainly. Romans dug the ditches with their spades and their masons laid the limestone pavings as it required some expertise. The guard who ran the quarry seemed to respond to Colin and began giving him a salute whenever he returned with the ox-cart and Colin wanted to join in and do his best. It was like his voluntary work with the Lions; camaraderie and hard work. Because of his size and reach he was an asset and the guard seemed keen to encourage him. It took about half an hour to load the cart, which was Colin's main task. On the first day his hands were scarred by the roughness of the stones and his skin dried by the lime. When they got back to camp one of the Britons looked at his palms and produced a small crock that was full of a paste that appeared to be grease and Colin recognised the smell as lanolin, which they washed out of sheep's wool, and herbs. By morning his hands were recovered, but he could not keep taking the man's potion. He showed Eiran the paste and the next night and they marvelled over it. Eiran and Dai were only used for digging ditches and laying sand for the base of the road. They did not need to handle the sharp slabs like Colin did. However they could speak to the other Britons and after a week one of them came to him to barter a pot of lanolin. Colin was not going to divulge he had a penknife. He used it for everything from cutting meat and bread to making gut and twine and whittling wooden items. He kept it in his pocket. It was his shirt, his jeans or his jumper. The man pointed at his shirt buttons. Colin was amused how the tribes people were fascinated by his shirt buttons. He had lost one or two but still had four and his cuff buttons. The man looked closely at the buttonholes and in the end they agreed to swap the liniment for four buttons, which left Colin with two to keep his shirt done up.

At night they sat around the camp fires listening to stories from other tribes and singing and playing rough music. He heard in their music the rhythms and memories from centuries of peoples long before the Romans came. He heard in the Roman camp the sound of bagpipes that he had seen at the camp last month but the Britons had only pipes and drums. He remembered the golden harp that the bard's servant carried and it's ethereal, heavenly sound. The pagan rites of the Britons seemed a million miles away from Cirencester.

When he was alone he had time to think about what they were doing. His vague recollections of history told him that this road would one day be called the Fosse Way, Fosse meaning ditch and ridge. He thought it went somewhere near Warwickshire. He assumed the Romans had already conquered England and he believed the north as well as where he stood was not colonised until later, maybe second century. The baths at Bath, Aquae Sulis, were probably already built. If the Fosse way was being built then Cirencester must already be a town. He wished he could see for himself. He had read books and seen movies but he still found it hard to believe that such huge buildings-temples and roads and bridges were already standing in this primitive landscape. He was surprised that the Britons were so nonplussed. Hadn't Boudicca led a rebellion and devastated Colchester and London by now? Did these Britons know anything about that? Why were they not fighting the Romans?

Round him the reasons were evident; the Romans brought occupation, industry and taught new skills. They were building roads. This brought trade and new ideas and people. He began to see why the elders of his tribe were so keen to put up markers of posts to lead the Romans to their village. They had something to give, a route over the Severn and access to Wales, not to mention the outcrops of iron bearing rocks. They could easily tempt the Romans to go that way. He could see that compared to their own mundane lives that was identical from year to year, the

Romans promised other possibilities such as jobs, training, work in villas and on farms, much better catered for than in his mud hut-dwelling colleagues by the Severn.

He imagined them being servants in a Roman household. They may be slaves even but they would have clothes, sandals, and even if they could not use the baths the house would have under floor heating in winter and food all year round. He thought the Romans had slaves not servants but maybe that was not correct in Britain at that time. If you had a decent master you might have a better life. The food would be more interesting too. Romans brought all their delicacies with them, sweet chestnuts, rabbits, grapes, cherries, dates and figs preserved, pickled fish and olives. Oil and most of all wine. By now they would have planted vineyards on the slopes of the downs in Kent and Sussex to make their own wine here.

Although Colin could not talk to the Romans he was almost able to pick out one or two words he recognised. He had done Latin at school but they did not seem to be speaking anything that sounded like Latin at all. If anything it sounded more like Greek which he had not studied at all. Certain syllables like "erion" as in cafeterion were apparent. He had tried to learn some Greek when he and Lesley were planning their honeymoon in Corfu. He also noted how different each Roman looked and were clearly from all parts of the Mediterranean. There were black people and some dark enough to have come from central Africa, others, lighter skinned, could have been from Tunisia or Egypt, others were clearly Scandinavian looking with blond, tow like hair and pale blue eyes. There were plenty of olive skinned types as he would expect but some were taller and brown haired with oval faces. He seemed to recall the busts of Roman emperors who were all different looking as well. Which emperor was in power now?

He thought Claudius had been emperor when they came to Britain followed by Caligula briefly but all that must be passed by. Hadrian had built his wall in the first century, to keep out the Picts and Constantine had been Christian about 300 AD. Maybe somewhere between 0 and 200 AD? He could not recall any other famous emperors between. He did know that Roman coins bore the heads of emperors though. What he needed to do was persuade a Roman to show him some coins and see if he could read the names on them. He trawled his memory about archaeology. He was sure that pre-Roman the Britons had coins as well yet he had never seen any change hands in the village not even when the salt seller came to sell.

The work was relentless. Colin had seen a couple of workers who were exhausted kicked out by the Romans. If you could not keep up with the two on/one off rota you were sacked. He noticed through the week several men arrived looking for work and the Romans took on every one. The Britons were under-nourished and could only work half as hard as the Romans but with tenacity they could build up muscle and strength as he was doing quite quickly. He assumed they had some form of pay and they wanted the roads built as fast as possible. As they reached the end of the ditches the land dipped towards the stream. More men were commandeered to dig a bigger causeway raising the road up. Then Colin was singled out with several others and marched forward with a platoon of about twenty Romans. They all now were in full kit and marched in order, the Britons coming up the rear looking like a rabble. They waded thigh deep across the shallowest part of the stream and headed towards the nearby hills. At the base were another group of soldiers and civilians who were removing scrub from an escarpment by burning. Colin was ordered to collect brush wood and fallen branches and heap them against the rock face. Eventually a large bonfire was erected and set fire up against the hillside. Colin was sent north with a party to get more wood and kindling. They made several journeys and he realised that without the road no ox carts could travel in this landscape so everything was done by manpower. He made three increasing journeys to the nearest forest with wood and on his last return, now getting dusk, he saw that the fires were burning low and the Romans were collecting water in leather skins from the nearest stream.

Colin was mystified by what they were doing. This was not a night fire; it was vast and the burning covered a large area of the hillside and laid bare the underlying limestone rock which was now charred it was so hot. Soldiers moved forward as a group and showered the rock with cold water. Colin jumped out of his skin as the whole area was filled with cracks and explosions as the hot stone shrank and contracted with the sudden cold. It finally dawned on him that this was the start of another quarry.

After dark they settled down to a poor dinner. Colin had nothing left of any food he had been given and all they were making was a sort of porridge with barley and water. He supposed working groups were on short rations and the Romans had their own picnic. He could see them using knives to eat dried meats, fruit and olives. The Britons were either too tired or too hopeless of catching anything to eat at this late hour. Colin fell asleep in his two sheepskins. He noticed some of the Romans were collecting hot stones from the escarpment to put in their bedding and he followed suit having a slab of hot limestone for his feet; the first time he had gone to sleep with warm feet for three weeks.

The following day they awoke at dawn, exhausted, but were ordered up by the Romans to get to work. As the sun rose they were allowed ten minutes for the Britons to hail the sun god, then were given picks and hammers to start working on the rock. The firing had exposed cracks in which they could get wedges and they worked downward from the top of the hill exposing more and more layers of limestone. Two more parties of Britons had been brought across the stream to work the limestone. They began to produce substantial quantities of flat slabs but Colin reckoned if they were going to Warwickshire they would need dozens of quarries worked for a year continuously.

Colin made a note that if he ever got back home he would walk up the Fosseway, albeit now a tarmac road, and shout "I built this" as he went. After a week of toil when more and more men arrived, thankfully bringing food, Colin was taken off quarry duty and told to go back to the new river bridge. He was amazed to see the Romans had diverted the stream by means of wood piles and were busy erecting a sort of wooden scaffold where the bridge would be. Carts would now come as far as the causeway and he noticed not slabs of limestone but huge squared off stones on each cart. Some were flat; others curved and beautifully cut. He could see the tool marks glistening along their sides. A party of Roman engineers were busy unloading posts and ropes and he was made to carry them into the stream bed. Being taller he was able to stand in deeper water so spent the next few days wading about and stabilizing what appeared to be wooden cranes and pulleys in the river bed. Slowly but methodically the Romans used a wooden causeway alongside the bridge position to roll the flat limestones into four fixed points. Cranes were then used to rope up the stones and lower them into place in the river bed. Each crane had its own party of Romans who roped, lifted and then winched the stones into pre-marked places until after a week there were four low piers in the bed of the river.

Most of the water had been diverted to the north but they were still working in two or three feet of water. Carts continued to arrive carrying more and more stones and Colin was awed to see each great rock manoeuvred into its position atop the piers. They had brought with them wooden templates to hold the curved stones in place for the arches and until the keystones were placed remained under the arches-eight in all. Once there were the bones of the bridge another party started building the causeway on the far side to raise it up to the level of the bridge. For once Colin felt inspired to keep working and for once could see the purpose of the task ahead of him. His work in the quarry had improved his musculature and now the Romans were bringing meat and cheese and good bread up to the site he was feeling stronger every day and able to work a ten hour day. He had never been so fit and healthy in his old life.

By the time the second causeway was raised up they had produced the dressed stones to form the top of the bridge which were solid limestones which fitted over the arches with a low parapet each side. The bridge was not the width of the road, about half the width he would guess but just wide enough for the ox carts to cross one at a time. After a couple of weeks the bridge was passable and the wooden template dismantled and carted up for the next bridge. The water of the stream was then released back into its original bed and the piles removed for use again. Colin was struck by the fact they had made a bridge capable of being used for hundreds of years ahead in just a few weeks when in his time such an enterprise would take months even with modern equipment and probably not be made of stone, which was too labour intensive and needed expert skills. But that was all they did have and an endless supply of labour and trained builders and navigators entering a land where no building work had ever taken place before.

CHAPTER 11

BACHANALIA

It had taken about three weeks to complete the bridge and about fifty to sixty men working continuously. They did not seem to have a day off either, working ten hours a day and seven days a week. He had begun to get to know some of the centurions as well. There was a short, stocky middle aged man who seemed very fair. He was strict and sent off two or three Britons who were not prepared to work hard but he appreciated Colin despite his natural slowness and seemed to recognise he was very different from his compatriots. Occasionally, when Colin was waiting for the oxen to be hitched he would talk to Colin, clearly trying to find out about him, to no avail. Colin could not even recognise even the most basic words they spoke. He wished he could talk. What stories they could tell! They must know all about doings in Rome, emperors, Cleopatra, Carthage, the slaughter of the Jews at Masada. They might have seen Rome when it was built, Jerusalem with the temple still there, the deserts of Northern Africa with vines and olive groves. He wished he could warn them of the Goths, but he guessed that was a couple of hundred years ahead. These men would never know defeat.

Another younger centurion who seemed more knowledgeable about bridge building, took to sitting near him at lunchtime. Colin asked by sign language and rough latin who was "imperator". Eventually the soldier brought out a leather bag that was a purse and showed him the coins. There they were the names and faces of the emperors. He could not make out much but one looked like CUN, another like CLA but it meant little to him. They would be killing Christians all over the Mediterranean soon. Good job he was not wearing a crucifix.

Every day they walked back down the road to the last fort, seven or eight miles, until the new fort before the bridge was in process. Then the Britons brought their skins and their poles and made a new encampment where the new fort may be. They bent hazel boughs over and covered them with skins to make a rough tent. It was warm enough to sleep in the open but there were intermittent showers every day so cover was preferable. Eiran, Dai Colin and Yarren combined their skins to make a shelter with its back to the south west where the wind came from. The weather in AD 50 was clearly much warmer. Colin had not arrived until September and it was quite hot then and now they were in early summer he found he could work bare chested in the day and to sleep in the thin wool tunic he used to cover his legs as they stuck out much further than the others.

In the morning they were provided with breakfast; bread and some sort of dried meat and dried fruits if they wanted them. He could not help feel that the Romans were giving them the worst of their supplies and why not? The Roman food was so strange to Britons that they would not appreciate the olive oil and sharp tastes of the pickles, onion and fish sauce but Colin was keen to access things he had sampled in his own life. In the day they served hot fishy soup with bread that tasted salty now he had got used to the bland fare of his tribe. Fortunately they were near the river so he could get plenty of water. The latrines were down river from the bridge so it was safe to drink water further up. He still did his own washing much to the amusement of Eiran and the others but since the fort was being built he noticed that the slaves were bringing clothes down to the river to wash as he did. The Roman dress seemed to be composed of a soft leather tunic under a breast and back plate with bare arms and legs. They had thick wool kilts and leather shoes with soles on them. He supposed in Britain that the dress was more suited to the climate. Roman sandals would not have fared well in the wet and muddy climate. He was surprised that the soldiers still wore their armour and were prepared to work as hard as the slaves and dug like fiends to raise up the causeway. Maybe they were paid piece work? The quicker the road was built the more they got paid.

After about twenty eight days from their arrival, one late afternoon, a party of soldiers came up the road and called out. The Britons were indicated to down tools and line up. A brawny, battle scarred soldier was handing out pay. Colin could see the purpose of their task. They could get currency with which they could buy things from the Romans. Colin was near the end of the line and saw them doling out coins and small twists of leather which he later discovered was salt. He would have been happier with something useful like a pair of shoes or another shirt. Twenty silver coins were given to him the same as all the others, and his twist of salt. Only the Britons were paid this way. He noticed some of them left the work party after this, but all the time small groups were coming up and asking for work. It reminded him of the navvies who were hired in the nineteenth century when they built the railways; there was always work for a strong and willing man. He put his silver coins into a left hand pocket and the salt with his bundle in the shelter.

The work ended earlier that day and Colin was aware that the Britons were looking more enthusiastic than they had before. He watched the Romans marching away down the road South and was surprised to see Eiran and Yarren and Dai washing in the river-naked. He followed suit as it was a warm afternoon, but instead of settling down for the night they indicated they would be following the Romans down the road. Colin had no idea where they were now. The Fosse Way led from Cirencester but did it go below as well? At what point were they? He guessed Cirencester was due south so was keen to see what lay ahead so followed willingly. It was now over ten miles back to Cirencester. A good three hours walk but it was a pleasure to be on the smooth sanded surface of the new road, up above the landscape, with no brambles and ditches to get caught up in. They swung along, Eiran singing a marching song, the others joining in now and then. After about two hours they sat down and ate some bread and found a small spring near the road. There were various parties going along south now; they were followed by people from the new quarry and the previous quarry until quite a large group, fifty or sixty men were all marching along the top of the road. It was a fine sight, the creamy limestone in diamond shaped slabs looked almost modern with a clever camber so that any rain washed off into the ditches either side. It appeared quite straight but Colin could not see any buildings other than the first fort they had camped by and the guard posts every mile. At least you knew exactly how far you had gone. One day they would set milestones at the side of the road, many of which were still visible in his day. He counted the posts, now empty and when he got to nine he could see the land dipping away towards the valley of the Colne. Colin was excited. This was the A417 again and on its way through Rendcombe a steep sided valley north of Cirencester.

Suddenly they could look down into the vale and the new city was before them. It was huge! Colin could see pallisades of wood and beyond one or two large stone buildings still being erected with pulleys and cranes to move the masonry. He could see many fires or forges inside the wall and many round huts encamped outside the pallisade busy with activities, children, women, washing on bushes and people tending cooking pots on open fires. This was what he had hoped to see all his time in the camp at Tewkesbury, a real Roman town.

The road ran straight up to a fortified entrance with a draw bridge over a massive ditch. Similar to the building at

Crickley Hill but more sophisticated. On the tower above the entrance were armed soldiers and from within he could hear the whinney of horses. As they streamed down the road Yarren and Eiran and Dai met with acquaintances they had seen before. Most people stared at Colin but he had got used to it by now. They climbed down from the road and began to join the hearths in the encampment outside the walls. After a while they sat down with a group Eiran seemed to know well and each of them handed over two silver coins for which they were given food and cider in plenty. They had been roasting a pig but there were Roman foods as well; lentils and barley with mushrooms and artichokes, anchovies and sardines, walnuts and different sorts of breads. There were odd cheeses some soft like cottage cheese others tart and goaty. There was good olive oil and wine and Colin began to feel the month's hard work was worth it. He had eighteen more coins each worth a days work so he was hoping for plenty from his hosts for all that amount of money.

He had begun to get tipsy with the cider when the party started. First some musicians arrived out of the town playing strange small bagpipes, flutes and drums, quickly followed by olive skinned women who danced and sang. They were fantastic to Colin's eyes, head dresses with coins jingling, fine silk robes which clung to their bodies and gold jewellery on their arms and fingers. The dyes and the colours were magnificent; blues and golds and cerise. They were a troupe of dancers that looked to him like gypsies, flashing their eyes and using their hands decoratively. He was mesmerised by the sounds and sights. Soon other women were walking among the fires, fine plump looking beauties, some with blonde hair and blue eyes, others with almond shaped eyes painted with kohl, slender girls like boys with long limbs clad in gold bindings. Colin noticed some of the men gesturing to the girls who were haughty and proud and he then realised they were prostitutes. In the light of the fires he caught sight of coins exchanging hands and suddenly he started to think of Sian. Could he betray her? He was quite overcome with drink and it seemed so easy to succumb to the bejewelled damsels.

One tall and Arabic looking girl took an interest in him and pulled him to his feet and she danced invitingly in front of him caressing his body with slender brown hands. Colin was struck still and dumb feeling like a great clod beside her. She gestured with her fingers for money. Colin looked round. There seemed to be no end of frolicking and grappling going on outside the firelight. In the end he produced one silver coin and she snarled back at him. Obviously these were high status hookers. He brought out one coin more and she gestured for more but he shook his head. She was speaking, selling her craft but it was wasted on Colin. He said no and she understood, two coins is all he would offer. She made to walk away and he put the coins back in his pocket. Clearly this was not what she was used to. He was not playing the game properly. Even he was not prepared to lose his hard earned cash with a confidence trick. In the end they compromised. He managed to say one coin now and one after in sign language and the woman, for she was no girl, got to work with Colin spread-eagled on his back while she demonstrated her craft. It was professional but nowhere so pleasant as Sian's gentle affection. Colin was seized by a desire to try something different and as he was paying he held her by the hair and pushed her down on her knees and took her from behind. To him this was something quite new but she played her part expertly, writhing about and pretending to be mastered. He gave her the second coin and she was soon off without even a goodbye. Colin was left on the ground feeling he had been ravished.

He fell asleep where he lay, making sure his other coins were still in his pocket, along with his penknife. Suddenly he was woken by a huge commotion of drums and chanting. There was some sort of ceremony going on alongside the river bank. He could make out the glow of a white pony and a dancing man wearing white robes. "Oh no not the bestiality again" he said out loud, but nevertheless wandered down the slope to watch. The Britons were grouped around an arena with the priest holding up some sort of wand. Several young girls were dancing in a troupe, around and around, swaying, bowing. He watched fascinated as the priest leaped in and out of their circle, the girls closing in on him, pawing and groping at him in their midst. Eventually to a crescendo of drumming he sank to the ground and was apparently overcome by the girls who yelped and whooped as they flailed their arms over him. There was a gasp and a cry, then their tune changed. Now they were wailing and gnashing their teeth, rending their robes. The crowd drew nearer, the drums getting slower and more insistent. He could see the priest lying as if dead and the girls now naked, mourning his demise. For a minute Colin thought they had actually killed him, he looked so still, then the music changed. A single flute sounded and a cymbal as the girls swayed over the priest he stirred and began to rise up. The crowd went mad with glee. Now Colin got it. Death and rebirth, Old man Barleycorn. Up sprang John Barleycorn-diddle diddle dol. And up sprang the priest and he reached out as if to catch one of the girls and squealing they ran off with him in pursuit. As they darted away other men caught hold of each of them and carried them away from the light.

The air was full of grunting and groaning. Like the priest the crowd were titillated and probably very drunk and all were turning to each other and coupling where they fell. After his encounter with the woman his desire was somewhat quenched but he did not want to be used by any other strange woman, as he saw it. He began to walk along into the darkness, away from the camp, along the river to get away from the orgy that was going on all around him. Over the palisade he could hear the same rabble swearing and howling on the Roman side. He could only imagine what exotic activities they were getting up to.

After about one hundred yards the palisade was nearer the river so he had to walk up to the posts. They were split trees held together by horizontal bars inside and there were cracks and gaps he could see firelight through. He looked round and saw no one else was there. He put his eye to a hole and peered in. In front was a small building open at the front with a counter for selling things. His eyes were getting used to the light and everywhere he saw depravity. Men and women were flailing about in twos and threes, limbs all over the place, first with this person then another, some in a sort of conga of sex. Colin was both repulsed and amazed. It reminded him of pictures of hell with firelight, naked bodies, screaming and twisting about.

After some time the noise seemed less and people were sitting, dazed and exhausted on the ground, women wandering off with their clothes rent and breasts exposed. Colin felt rather grubby and embarrassed. He made his way back to where the fires were. The Britons were continuing their own orgy outside the palisade, in the dark and more mundane than the Roman erotica. He could not recall where he had left his skin roll and possessions and had to wander about in the dark trying to remember which fire they had been sitting at. It was hopeless. Everything was tossed about and disturbed and he could not recognise any possessions any more. He curled up near a fire and fell into a deep sleep to the whimpering and moaning of all around him.

When dawn broke most of the Britons were asleep on the ground. Colin saw the beams over the horizon; a hilly region covered in low trees and bushes. The priest appeared and gathered a small group around him, chanting and swishing his wand about for the sunrise ceremony. Colin stood up and raised his arm along with the others. He felt stiff, chilled and damp and rather wished he had not taken part at all. Now he had lost all his bedding, his wool tunic, his salt, drinking flagon and calendar stick. As the sun rose he went back to where he had descended from the road and tried to guess where the hearth was where they had eaten. Eventually he found Yarren sitting on a tussock holding his head and Colin went to get him some water in Yarren's flagon, but he looked the worse for wear. However he did then spot the familiar tied bundle that was his skins and tunic although the salt had been taken and the flagon.

Such is life. He had had an experience he would never have known in his past life; what was there to lose but a few trinkets? He checked his pockets and still had his silver coins and his pen knife. He went to the river, washed, and sat by the glittering water until people were up and about. He was starving now and wondered if he had to pay for breakfast as well. However his previous night's coins seemed to have done the trick and eventually two young girls came with honey cakes, cheese and dates. Colin assumed that somehow the children were protected from the orgy. There were tents alongside the palisade and small children were now playing outside in the sun. A young mother breast fed her baby within her shawl. Colin felt a pang of guilt and longing for Sian. He did not know but she must be six months pregnant by now, quite large he would think. How he wanted to hold her close and feel his baby moving. Why had they taken him away as soon as she was in need of him? Eventually Eiran, Yarren and Dai got themselves together and ate breakfast.

Clearly they were not going to be working today. No Romans appeared outside the town. Shortly Colin saw some of the Romans coming among the Britons. They were salesmen selling all manner of jewellery, pots, leather goods, clothes, ornaments and weapons. Colin did not trust himself to buy anything, not knowing the value of his coins. Soon he saw the young centurion from the bridge coming towards him. He was in his part-armour but with no helmet. He held up his hand in greeting and indicated the camp grinning.

Colin knew he was asking him if he enjoyed the evening entertainments so he gave the thumbs up sign. The centurion looked at him startled. Clearly thumbs up did not mean the same thing in Latin. Despite his surprise he indicated they could go to the gate. Colin was intrigued. He did not feel scared even though he knew to go off without his friends spelled danger, but the young man seemed genuine. They climbed up on to the road and walked over the draw bridge. Saluted by the guard, Colin was going to see inside the town after all.

It was mainly a building site, everywhere there were cranes and hoists, huge wooden structures to lift and move masonry. A whole area was given over to masons, the air still thick with dust although no one was working today. He saw the beginnings of statuary and columns, some Roman letters being cut into a plinth. The most organised part of the town were the shopping streets, three or four of which ran parallel with booths, some covered over with cloths, some open selling breakfast. Strange strong smells assaulted his nostrils; amphorae with wine and ladles, crocks of olives and dried fruit, platters of nuts, hot cakes, flat breads, pieces of pastry and patties of meat. Jars of silver fishes in oil, stews in cauldrons over ovens. They walked along streets of food sellers and leather workers, harness makers, carpenters and iron workers; a stall selling polished stones and silver jewellery, bone combs and hair decoration. A scribe selling his skills to write documents, an apothecary with piles of ores and powders, unguents and scents. Colin could not think of anything he wanted to buy; he would like some shampoo, some shaving foam and some more of that lanolin hand cream for his blisters but could not recognise anything. His friend took him along the back of the town into a room with murals all round the walls. Colin suddenly realised they were pornographic and waved his hands in a negative gesture. All the men there laughed at him but he was not going to lose any more money.

Eventually he was shown the temple, still having a roof erected. There were white limestone steps up to the front and eight columns with floral decorations at the top and blank walls of stone. Inside there were more columns and the floor was being laid out. There was a stack of marble slabs that were being laid around the outside edges and along the walkway, which led to another doorway within. Inside the inner chamber was a plinth covered in letters and on top a painted stone figure, a woman holding a snake. He wished he had listened in Latin class. Athena had an owl but she was greek; he tried to think who was the Roman equivalent but it escaped him. His friend approached an old man in a rough gown. He was asking for some service and Colin saw him draw out a small pouch of stones. At first he thought they were runes but they had small dots like dice. Romans would have thought runes very suspicious no doubt. Dragging his memory he believed he had heard the Romans had driven the druids out of Britain but they all seemed to be rubbing along together at present. Had he not heard a story that druids sacrificed babies? He had seen some strange rites but no one got killed and all their practises seemed logical to him. It made sense to leave corpses for animals and birds to consume and then just bury the bones. Modern societies buried their dead and then kept the ashes.

The necessity of times bred the cultures of disposal. He wondered if sometime in the future even urns of ashes would be considered an extravagance and people would just have a compressed carbon bead to remember their ancestors.

His friend was pleased with his oracle and clapped Colin on the shoulder, grinning. Colin felt an urge to communicate his own expectations and pointed to his chest then mimicked the rocking movement of a baby. His friend understood and looked impressed. He pointed down and raised a finger "Now?" Colin held up his fingers, one, two, three months. He knew it did not make sense but his friend looked pleased for him. He drew him away from the temple towards the forum laid out ahead of them. Many robed men, not soldiers, strolled about, were gathered in groups talking, sitting, arguing. To the end of a great paved square was a well, a newly built masonry wall was built about it with steps going up and two or three women kneeling and praying. Above the well was a statue, half kneeling, half crouching with a ewer in her arms. The source of water fell from the ewer into the well and Colin was mesmerised by the glistening purity of the goddess and the water, springing from whatever source in the middle of the town.

The centurion led Colin to a stall where small pieces of lead like luggage labels were being sold. He was encouraged to draw out his precious coins and got some dull bronze ones instead of his shiny silver one and a dull leaden tablet. He was offered a stylus with a sharp end and indicated to scratch on it. Colin suddenly understood; he was to scratch a message on the tablet and toss it into the well. He set about writing "may Sian be delivered of a healthy child", curled it up into a roll and with his wish threw it over the lip as he looked at the goddess. He no longer knew what day it was having lost his calendar stick and felt all at sea, but he prayed she was not yet due and he longed to be back in time to see his child born.

They stopped at a booth and ate some meatballs and flatbread washed down with wine. The Romans around him stared and commented on this tall fair man amongst them and joked with the centurion about his possession. They did not drink strong wine and to Colin it seemed very weak especially compared to the strong cider favoured by the Britons. It felt very modern to him, like a day in Cheltenham sitting in the promenade on a sunny day. People relaxing, various races and tongues, exotic foods and the odd vehicle passing by. He saw no chariots but there were horse drawn carts in the town. He had not seen any horses in the camps he passed only oxen but the Romans seemed to have many. Everywhere there were busy salesmen with carts and barrows bringing in more and more goods for sale. It was a holiday and after pay day there was plenty of business going on.

At about midday they shook hands and he set off to find Eiran, Yarren and Dai. They were sitting with their acquaintance at the hearth which was now smouldering, not drinking cider, but water from their flagons. Colin joined them thoughtfully. It was strange being able to live out the fantasy he had dreamed of since he had been whisked off to another time. The Romans, the soldiers, the food, the fabulous masonry and industriousness they demonstrated was everything he expected. True it was mostly a building site but Corinium, as he knew this to be, was no disappointment.

CHAPTER 12

MIDSUMMER

Colin had lost track of time. When he had had his bark and string calendar he knew within a few days or so where he was in the year. It was his last little bit of sanity in a life that had gone completely beyond his control. At least he should be grateful he had not been enslaved, tortured or murdered. All in all the tribe had been exceptionally good to him. Feeding him and bedding him in a world where a couple of extra weeks of snow was the difference between life and death.

He reckoned they had got to the Fosseway about the 24th March. Since then his endless slogging away in the quarry and relentless working dawn to dusk, which was now getting longer and longer, he had been unable to record how many days he had been away from the village. Clearly the Bachanalia he witnessed last week must correlate to some pagan date. It must be May already. The bracken was shooting up through the bluebells. He always remembered that sight on Bank Holidays in the woods. So was last week the 1st of May? He decided to start making a record again, but on what? It had to be miniaturised. He recalled native americans who seemed to make cuts on sticks. He could do that too. While in the quarry he had found some hazel boughs and cut off a piece about a centimetre wide and two feet long. He should be able to get three months on one side then use the other side for the next three months. He could not imagine staying in this worksite another three months let alone six. The twenty little silver coins he had earned were hardly worth the effort, wine and oysters or not.

The bridge was now almost completed with its span resting on the arches of limestone. It sparkled in the sun and never had he felt so proud of something he had created. At one end the Romans were beginning to dismantle the wooden scaffolding that had supported the stonework and were loading it on to ox carts, no doubt to be used again at the next building work.

He wished so hard he could get back to his own life just to be able to say "I built the Fosseway". Yarren had visibly grown since they left the village, his muscles were filling out with the better food and hard work and his broad back was tanned with ten hours a day bare-chested outside. His beard was beginning to show brown and curly, more dense than Colin's. When he returned home Colin thought he would be a good catch for the village girls. How he missed Sian though. It had been about seven weeks since he left and wondered if she was showing his child yet. The more he thought the more he guessed she was three months gone in

February. She would be six months gone now, well on the way. A slow desire was growing in him to be with her and share the growth of his baby. But would he see her again?

What was stopping him just walking away and going back home? He did not think he would get lost either. He would just make his way north and west of Crickley Hill and find a route across flat land to Tewkesbury. But somehow the bond with Eiran and Yarren and Dai was strong and he would feel he was betraying them in some way if he left. He did not know what had been agreed with the Romans either. Were they bound by a contract or just earning their keep?

He was fascinated by everything the Romans did, even so. Every mile along the road they built an outpost with a palisade of wood and a tower from which they sent signals to the next post and so on down the line. They did not need horses to carry mail they had flags and torches and even a form of semaphore using a slide machine and a light. Every ten forts they built a bigger one like Cirencester. Within a fortnight they had latrines that spilled out straight into the river and were in the process of building a bath house with under floor heating. They set up all their manufacturing on site; carpenters, builders, stone masons, engineers, signalmen, cleaners, tile makers, and potters. Then there were the service staff, horsemen, messengers, and cart drivers. Tool menders, weavers and clothiers, cooks, vintners, shop keepers and leatherworkers. All these people had to be fed and sometimes paid, yet up the paved road came cart after cart of supplies. Dried fruits, pickled vegetables, nuts, oil and wine; spices and herbs and above all salt. They brought their own sheep, goats and pigs and much to the amusement of locals the chickens that were tame and scratched about everywhere and produced endless supplies of eggs. Colin was never so happy to see the Romans arrive with their culinary expertise. But he was restless too. They were building the road north, creating the Roman Empire.

He could not recall where the Fosseway went, Warwickshire somewhere, that was a long road to build. Would he see it all the way up? He wanted so much to march back down it to wherever it led south. To Roman towns maybe Bath or Dorchester? Could he have a life there? Could he make a living and take Sian with him? Would he become one of the first Romano British?

Colin's fears of being stuck on the road to Warwick were not wholly founded but it was another three weeks before he discovered their plans. On the second month when they were paid Eiran attracted his attention. In the mud he drew the Fosseway, Cirencester and the road south. He pointed at the south route, at Colin and Yarren and indicated that they would walk down it. Colin took some moments to understand but in repeating the finger walking sign and pointing south he was greeted with nods from the others. They were on the move again. The plan was and presumably always had been to go south. Colin felt torn. He knew he should go back to Sian but the excitement of discovering a Roman City was too much to give up. He looked at Eiran and made a cradling motion with his arms and pointed north. Eiran knew straight away what he meant and held up three fingers. Then he indicated Colin returning up the road to Tewkesbury and making a round belly gesture. Colin realised he knew what Colin worried about and was saying that Sian was not due for another three months and they would return by the time she was big bellied. Colin felt all the less guilty for knowing this and pleased that Eiran had a plan that involved going home this year. He guessed they would not want to be away in winter. Maybe they had to return for harvest anyway.

Colin fell to his tasks with more vigour now he could plan out his summer. It was late May and a period of particularly sunny weather meant they could bathe in the river, above the latrines, and lie on the bank to dry. Colin wondered what he could do with his few silver coins. What were they worth? He had been working for two months so they must be valuable but he had also been fed and given wine and salt as part of his wages so maybe it was just pin money? Even if he was ranked just above slave the others were working for the same amount.

The road increased by about a 100 yards a day. It was so well organised. The sappers went ahead, chopping down trees, clearing land and digging great ditches either side to build up the causeway. Then the road builders layered gravel and sand to make a bed for the stone. The masons laid the slabs and in turn they accessed the site by driving up the road, and any defects were repaired by road menders immediately.

Colin could see how important their planning and geography needed to be otherwise they could be heading away from the next bridge and wasting time and effort re-routing the road.

Eventually he had added twenty one more notches on the calendar stick and reckoned it was about 28th May.

At home they would be looking forward to the May Bank Holiday. There would be a fair on the Abbey field, a charity cricket match, the vicar would arrange guided tours of the tower of the Abbey. Colin went every year. He loved to be up so high and to be able to gaze over the river, May Hill and the blue hills of Wales beyond. Last year he had just passed his driving test and took Lesley to the Wye Valley for a picnic. He had been idyllically happy. They sat in the grounds of Tintern Abbey eating peanut butter sandwiches listening to the transistor radio and planning their future. Lesley wanted two boys; he wanted one of each. They would be married at Saint Antony's, the Abbey was far too costly and neither had been religious although they had been going to church occasionally to make it look good. Colin's mum would be making roast beef and his dad would be at the cricket ground or the Conservative club. On Monday they had been used to going out in the car-usually to Malvern or Hereford shows- but as Colin grew older they gave this up. Colin began to wonder what he had been doing for the last nine years. He had got his O levels, gone to work in the bank and taken his driving test and that was about it. In the last six months he had learned to fish for his life, improvise many tools, sew sheepskins, smelt iron, grind barley and oats, cook, make love, hunt boar and wrens, learned about pagan religious rites as well as quarry limestone and build roman roads.

He wondered why he had wasted so much of his life so far. Maybe the Britons, having a shorter lifespan, just made the most of it quicker. Look at Sian, pregnant at fifteen. In his world that would be frowned upon and yet it was the most worthwhile thing she could have done. Lesley could take a leaf out of her book instead of running off to London with a third rate rock musician. There was no excitement about the town so Colin guessed there was no celebration now at the end of May. Everything passed as usual. A priest of some sort came to the 10 mile fort in a sedan chair carried by six slaves. They were big men who looked German to Colin. The fort was finished and the routine of military life was in full flow. Outside the fort about fifty feet away the Romans were putting in place foundations for a large oblong building. Slaves came up in droves from the south and soon were using the quarry that Colin worked in to obtain the harder, less exposed limestone. He saw the first blocks arrive, oblong chunks loaded on to ox carts and one by one pushed into place by rolling logs and ropes and pulleys.

The priest came out of the fort with many acolytes carrying great bronze trays and tripods for burning incense. They set up inside the foundations and the soldiers were present to witness the rituals. Among cymbals and smoke they brought forward a goose, a hen and a goat. All of them were ritually slaughtered, much to Colin's distaste, their guts and blood examined by the priest for omens. It appeared the omens were good and the site propitious, as the soldiers hailed Caesar then left the slaves and engineers to carry on the building.

Colin had spent much time listening to and trying to converse with the Romans and slaves. Some of the slaves clearly spoke foreign languages other than Roman but he hardly recognised any Roman words from his Latin knowledge. He had never listened in Latin lessons being of the view he would never need it; but now the odd word sounded familiar and after a few weeks the same phrases said over and over stuck in his mind. "Get those oxen moving", "Hurry up", "Do you want this food?" "Get your own water", "Take this and get on with it", "Make bigger slabs", "Stop work, everyone back to camp". These seemed to ring in his ears several times a day. No doubt there were plenty of Roman words for "dickhead", "idiot" or "scum" but he could not discern the difference.

June began, the weather turned wet and windy and they were caught in a mire of lime dust and soggy top soil. Colin was commandeered to help finish the parapet of the bridge, using block and tackle and they shifted block after block from the oxcart up to the next layer until about three feet of wall stood proud of the road. The slaves mixed lime mortar to seal the slabs but Colin was impressed with the accuracy and immaculate measuring that produced such a stunning bridge. Nothing had been seen in Britain like this before but Colin had seen photos of the Bridge at Avignon and how grand a scale the Romans could build on. This was peanuts in comparison. It had taken about twenty men about a month to finish this bridge over a river with a span of about twenty feet yet it might remain here for two thousand years if no one knocked it down.

After about three days the rain subsided and the ox-carts trailed back and forth to the quarries day in and day out. The Romans were clearly dejected when it rained and went about their tasks like whipped dogs with leather cowls over their uniforms. They appeared to work three shifts a day either guarding the fort or supervising work, sleeping or hanging about drinking wine and preening themselves in the baths. The bath house was in progress but it would be months before it would be finished as the slaves were mainly occupied with the bridge or temple. Colin watched as Romans tried to persuade Britons to join the labour force. There must be some agreement with local chiefs not to upset the local natives, Colin thought, at least until the roads were built, or why not just enslave them as well? He supposed it would cause too much friction and they could not spend all their time fighting when they needed to get the country organised and under their control. They were here to build a nation not get involved in tribal squabbles. If the Britons wanted to go on making pots and jewellery, let them. Those who offered to make Roman tiles for roofs and bath houses soon found they were getting rich and growing in status over their own folk. Soon tile makers were drinking wine and wearing embroidered goat skin coats, roman sandals and shaving their beards off.

The Romanisation of Britain was by willing acolytes not by force. The chief of Cirencester region had clearly agreed to all this building in what had been his settlement. He must be expecting rewards beyond his dreams to persuade his people to agree to this. True, the Romans were building downstream in the lower valley of the river Colne but one day Roman Cirencester, Corinium as it was then known, would wipe out the round huts and wooden halls of the Britons. They had to join or go under; best to back the winning side.

After a week of unsettled weather in June it began to get warmer and sunnier. Colin thought that in a couple of weeks it would be the longest day, then their working hours would gradually diminish again. He wondered how they managed in winter. Did they use torches and work through the dark evenings? How did they manage at Hadrian's wall where the days would have been only a few hours in winter?

To him the work seemed to be extraordinarily speedy. How could they keep up such a pace? The soldiers and slaves worked together and the Britons joined in with the heavy work but all worked as one. It was not so much they were threatened or beaten but the relentless organisation of the work force that achieved this goal. Every man knew what he was doing at any time and had the right tools to complete his task. Each knew that at a given time he would have a break and that he would be fed at the end of the day. Colin laughed at the comparison with workmen in his world. Not only did workmen seem to be continually on strike but when they were working it was work to rule and down tools if one was picked on for being lazy. The British workman had gained the reputation of leaning on his spade drinking tea and claiming they could not carry on due to some trivial hold up.

Here there was no consideration given to weather or conditions in mud or dust but then the British climate was fairly moderate so they were not made ill by heat or cold or extreme conditions. The centurions in charge missed nothing but they were fair. If any man started to flag they were chided back into their stride and if they continued to lose continuity they were thrown off. At one point a dark skinned man was staggering with his load at unloading the cart. He was detailed off and sent back down the road with a civilian worker. Colin wondered if he was a slave what would happen? Would he be treated or beaten? If a slave could not work were they killed?

Colin had built up so much muscle the daily grind did little to tire him and he usually swam in the river for half an hour after work each day, making use of the last warmth of the evening. No one swam. Both Romans and Britons alike were intrigued by his swimming techniques and he enjoyed showing off his different strokes and lying on top of the water. Most of the fishermen could stay afloat by splashing and flapping about but Colin's cool overarm followed by back stroke up the centre of the river amazed them. He felt proud that at least there was one thing he could do better than the Romans.

One warm night in June when they finished Eiran called him over and taking his calendar stick and indicated that within three days they would be moving south. All four were to go. He did ask Colin if he wanted to come but Colin did not want to be left behind or return home alone. He felt these men knew what they were doing and would eventually get him home. If he stayed with the Romans there was no knowing how they might change. He could end up as a slave after all and once he was he could be transported anywhere in the world.

Three days later Eiran came to him and indicated he wanted four of the little silver coins. Colin trusted him wholeheartedly so he was not surprised that Eiran returned with a whole heap of goodies. He brought five water skins, three filled with wine; almost a basket full of dates stuffed with almonds and two jars of olives. There was salt pork, salt duck, fried chicken, eggs, goats cheese wrapped in leaves, olive oil, lamps with wicks, tinder boxes, a wooden pipe for playing tunes on. A spoon, a bottle of scent, a razor for Colin and two wax tablets for writing on. New sheepskins, a goatskin for himself and some arrows for Yarren. Each of them packed away as much as they could carry and Colin looked forward to the next morning.

When it came it was quite sad. He had worked beside slaves, paid workers and Romans alike and they were all work mates to him. His overseer, despite being curt and disciplined, had been fair and clapped his shoulder with good luck wishes. The slaves touched their heads in respect. Each had saved each other from a rock fall, a broken foot, falling in the river a dozen times and the bonds were strong.

Soon Colin and the others were marching south down the white paved road. They passed the water meadows of South Cerney and the first day they camped on the river at Lechlade. Although they had as much food as they could carry, Yarren still snared some hares and they ate an old fashioned stew again. The next day they reached a fort south of Cirencester. In a steep little valley the Romans were building houses and baths, temples, stables and were flooring a central forum between the buildings. Colin saw soldiers who were much more high status than their friends back at Cirencester, they wore red kilts, had bare legs and sandals and on duty wore plumed helmets and armour. There were Roman women too with braided hair and makeup. Along the back of the forum were stalls being laid out and one or two already had shopkeepers selling wine and oil and dried fruits. They even saw them planting a vineyard. There was a proper butchers area for cutting up meat with a great ox head hanging on a hook on the wall.

Further along farmers were curing hides, pummelling the leather in troughs and preparing dyes. They walked about entranced, for Yarren and Eiran these were all new sights. For Colin it was like being on the film set for Cleopatra. Everywhere there were drains and gutters on buildings, doors, and always in sight the white, white road stretching over the hill south.

Colin and the others camped with their fellow Britons further up stream. There was a great deal of excitement and chatter between the different tribes people who looked anxious and fearful of all these new concepts of living. The difference between the indigenous peoples and their bio-degradable lifestyle and the Roman immortality of their culture was shocking. A tribal camp could be abandoned and within twenty years the wind and weather would have decimated the reed roofs and wood frames, melted the wattle and daub and left nothing of the village except a pile of organic debris. Only the occasional post hole or trace of a hearth would remain for future archeologists. Here were towns that would be used for centuries and whose remains would last for millenia.

The sheer numbers of immigrants moving into Britain would surely put a stress on supplies. He could see sheep grazing all over the land up to the woodland and chickens were scratching everywhere. Goats were in pens behind every shop and house and long hunting dogs lounged in doorways. Cirencester would soon look like this, then Chester and Carlisle, all over Britain the massive building machine would go on and on, the British tribes would be pushed back further into the wild areas of Wales and Lancashire, unless they chose to join in and become Roman citizens. They would be powerless to fight back, the weapons and numbers of Romans would simply overwhelm them at first strike. These were people you did not argue with. The Romans were very careful not to upset the locals either. They let them carry on their religions and culture, made way for their festival days and did not go near the henges and sacred sites. Their roads skirted sacred mounds and ritual walkways. One day the advent of so many grazing animals would decimate the forests and the amount of timber taken for buildings would see large tracts of land opened up for occupation. Still the Britons would retain their little hilltop camps and posts where possible not realising they were a dying breed.

Yarren and Eiran spent a whole day talking with local people and it was clear there was some sort of stirring and some families were packing with their children the odd ox-cart for a journey. It reminded Colin of the trip to the Malverns for the Solstice ceremonies. The second day they bought more bread, cakes and another skin of wine; they had shared most of this with their friends; the second time Colin had felt drunk that year. They set off next day feeling rather hung over but cheerful. The route now was easier as the road ran down hill from the Cotswolds to rich river meadows. The air was full of flying insects chased by swallows and Colin began to regret the heat for being incessantly bitten where his flesh was exposed. They gathered certain herbs and rubbed them on their skin leaving a green residue but it did seem to discourage the midges.

They met Romans travelling along the road, soldiers on horses, soldiers marching, supply carts driven by slaves, parties of artisans and entertainers, all moving north. While their roads existed many would be drawn along the routes in preference to marshes and dense woodlands. There had been tracks around Tewkesbury though. He wondered if the poles they had erected on Bredon, Leckhampton and Crickley hill were to chart out a new route between their encampments, but Tewkesbury's main thoroughfares were rivers not roads.

Nightfall now was at 10pm and after a rest around dinner time and making a bonfire a good number of travellers seemed to be appearing from all directions and joining them. There were quite young children, women and all folk except Romans, tagging along, talking, laughing and eating snacks as they went. After dinner instead of making a camp Eiran urged Colin to pack up, stop eating olives and nuts and get to his feet. It was night yet they planned to keep up the march. It was pleasant enough, there was a moon and the air was almost warmer than the day. A slight breeze cooled their exertions as they clambered up a steep chalk escarpment whose track way was rutted and stony from erosion. Once up on the ridgeway Colin could see it was a vast upland plain devoid of trees for its thin chalky soil and across the land, lit up by moonlight, was the white scar of the track leading south and east.

All the travellers started to move faster, now not dawdling and chatting as before. The moon made its steady progress across the sky then set in the west a deep gold. The stars were an immense sea from that upland view and Colin was marching along staring above him when he became aware they were on the top of a slope downwards again and the travellers began to murmur and gasp at the view. Initially, his pupils, having been reduced by the light Colin could only see the darkness ahead. The ground ahead seemed to have low bushes or outcrops all over it which to him seemed to be moving. Yes they were definitely moving. It took Colin some moments to realise that these outcrops were actually the heads of seated people. Dozens, hundreds, no thousands of seated people all the way down the grassy slope as far as the eye could see. He was overwhelmed. How could so many people join together in this sparsely populated land? How could Eiran and the others have known how to get here all at the same time? As his eyes became accustomed to the dark he saw in the distance some torch light and recognised some ceremony was taking place, although it must be half a mile away. He realised the flames were going behind dark shadows; tall unreal shadows which partially reflected the light. His eyes became more accustomed to the deep darkness and he could make out a priest, no several priests, with their golden sickles and flowing robes behind the crowds of onlookers and Colin could see an altar lit by lamps and approached by various of the priests.

There was an air of excitement and expectation but only a murmur of voices and the odd cry of a child. Everyone seemed to be holding their breath. A voice raised above the murmur and the light sound of the breeze. It was a drone, a chant, coming from some gutteral part of the priests, inhuman and unworldly. Colin saw the flash of a stroke, an animal cried out and there was movement behind the shadows. The crowd muttered and gasped; more chanting and crying out ensued. It was only when he noticed the torch appear and disappear behind obstructions that he realised these were not buildings but the great stone circles of Stonehenge.

It was so obvious now he looked properly. The great vertical stones were capped all round with horizontal ones and above it was dark with some sort of covering. He could only see the ceremony through the stones at the sides. There must be some sort of roof over the whole edifice. As he was trying to define the outline of this original henge he heard the crowd begin to whisper and move about, heads all turning as one to the left. Colin stood open mouthed. He was tugged by Yarren to make his way to a slight promontory where they sat down above the endless audience of Britons. A low murmur rose up around them of children, of babies crying, of women whispering. Yet all heads were turned to the ceremony below. It was hard to make out what was going on. There were no ponies or other animals but a priest figure was flailing in the centre of the circle with what looked like a sickle in his hand. Suddenly the fire and torches were extinguished and a gasp rippled among the crowd.

Colin was probably the last to notice but there, discernable over the eastern horizon, higher than where they were sitting, was the first glimmer of the rising sun-midsummer was here. He waited, almost unable to breathe and the crowd gasped and started to rise. Colin looked east and yes, there on the farthest horizon was the faintest ray of gold. As those at the front rose the ones behind gradually stood, like a wave rolling back through the throng. He, at 6" to 8" above the others, could see over all. He was entranced how the glimmer became beams, a golden ribbon, faster and faster it began to glow until it burst through a slight V shape in the centre of the hills with a ray of white light entering the stones from the left touching the altar stone in the centre. There was a sigh and a groan, as of climax, as the crowd, as one, recognised the hand of their God reaching out to them and as one they saluted as all did in the sun service in all the camps in the land.

Never had Colin felt so at one with nature. This great power source that he took so much for granted about which he knew so much from doing science at school was still a source of awe and wonderment to these people. And they were right; no sun, no life; no crops, no fodder, no animals, no humans. Even for brief respites of sunlight people became morose and cold and miserable. No wonder they praised the sun rise and wished it well on its journey to the underworld at night. The moan kept going for about three minutes during which time more and more rays appeared over the horizon and surprisingly quickly there was light.

CHAPTER 13

BATH

The ceremony was a joyous outpouring of gratitude and respect for the sun god. Everyone was cheering and shouting and clapping each other on the back. Children woken from slumber as to a new world. Colin felt happy himself but wished he had been able to enjoy this moment with Sian. He wondered what the village people were doing on this day. The circle in the woods was not designed for sun worship and they went there in the dark to inter the dead and invoke spirits. This ceremony felt like a different religion altogether, clean and wholesome. There was no alcohol or orgies and gradually the people began to move slowly towards the stones in a loose unhurried column.

A procession of Britons approached the circle, some on horseback who dismounted before entering the stones. They appeared to be anointed by the priest and Colin guessed they were the hierarchy of priests and chieftains of tribes. The ceremony would confirm and strengthen the people's understanding of power and leadership. These men who were revered and singled out on this day were to be feared and obeyed because they were being blessed by the sun God.

There was more ceremony to come. Beyond in the far distance towards the sun was the sacred walkway, lined with standing stones, alternately vertical and round. Colin noted that the priests who had been within Stonehenge were now starting a procession along a pathway to the south east and with torches still lit led the people onwards to further celebrations. He was one of the last to join the endless stream of families and tribespeople on to a straight passage of about three miles towards the river there.

The sun rose and rose, an orange star burst in the night sky. Although it had been dark and cloudy they seemed to melt in the warmth and above them the green, then the blue arc expanded. All around he could hear sedge birds piping and as the sky lit up, the sweetness of larks rising. Truly this was an ecstasy of nature that all the people were part of on this day. It made him feel stupid in his twentieth century life for all its technology and arrogance, nothing invented could out power the sun. And where would he have been at such a time? Fast asleep in his bedroom which looked west anyway. Had he never got up to see the midsummer before? Getting up, going to work, wearing a suit, driving a car, all these things seemed so trivial compared to the life of his present companions. Living, surviving, breeding, welcoming, cherishing, cultivating, relishing. These were the preoccupations of the Britons, close to the earth, worshipping the sun and making history. He loved the intensity with which they absorbed everything around them and vowed if he got back he would never take for granted the basics of life, plants growing or a field of corn, fresh water and animals were all to be treasured and desired not just polluted and abused at will. He wanted so much to share this feeling with Sian and bring up his child in this way.

As the light grew and the chieftains left Stonehenge in the distance he caught a glimpse of another henge, this one on the flat river meadows and built of wood. It took about two hours to make their way to the grounds and already people had dispersed around the second henge.

They stood about watching queues of people entering the sacred avenue, families, women, children, old people, all slowly walking or being carried along the way. An old lady on a stretcher who looked almost dead. A woman in a blue shawl breast feeding a baby, a man stopping to tie a shoe. They walked and walked slowly going down hill to the river.

The second henge was wooden, made of great felled trees and put in a circle hundreds of feet across. In the centre was a wooden structure on stilts surrounded now by the druid priests and chieftains. Colin noticed people were approaching with what appeared to be bags of rags which were placed on the pyre. Colin felt he was watching some ritual on the Ganges in India. The white and yellow robes, the incense burning and the sun burning down on them reminded him of sites wholly foreign and from a different culture altogether. He worked out that the bundles contained bones which families had brought with them to give their ancestors' souls a pathway to the gods.

After about two hours, when Colin had fallen asleep, he woke up to an increasing wailing sound and saw that they had lit the pyre, its black smoke curling furiously up towards the sun which was now above them. The priests were moving around the henge now and he recognised the ceremony this time; it was the bone gathering he had seen in the village and he witnessed the bards with their gold sickles releasing the staked bones within this henge and reverently putting them into linen cloths.

All around the area were new raised barrows; some bald still and some grass grown. The priests were moving towards a new barrow, clearly built for this ceremony. It was vast, about a hundred feet long with new turf laid over the underlying structure and a shallow ditch dug out all around except the front where the curious double doors he had seen before were erected. The bones in their sheaths were taken one by one by priests, blessed with boughs of green and oils and carried solemnly into the dark underground passage. Colin knew from TV that the inside would have had sections like small rooms and the bones laid in special order according to some religious mores. Eventually the whole of the mound would be buried in soil and covered over, to be plundered throughout history by tribes whose memories recalled the treasures they expected to be buried there. Rarely were goods buried and in the twentieth century the British barrows were found devoid of anything but bones. Whether stolen or absent it was hard to know.

Later as the centuries passed the Saxons and Vikings would bury their dead with fabulous jewels, metalwork and weapons that could be found. Recently Colin had been reading about Sutton Hoo, believed to be a Viking burial where not only were the grave goods spectacular but also his horse and chariot had been buried with the chief or king. Vikings had also buried their chiefs under river beds to stop pillage so he assumed that plenty of burials would be left to be excavated long into the future.

After the interment of the bones it was full morning and the sun shone hot. The people in their thousands sat on the grass around the henge picnicking with breads and cheese, dried meats and fruit. Eiran and Dai had urged them to use their silver coins to buy more food at the last settlement and Colin was feasting on some sort of pie with meat filling, stuffed vine leaves and olives, drinking wine and sweet honey cakes. Whatever the reason for this ceremony he felt the exuberance all around within the people.

From now on the crops would flourish. Young animals born in the chill of spring would thrive and grow large on the abundant fodder available, fattened up for the winter kill. There would be grain and straw and hay and beans for everyone as long as the rains rained and the sun shone. Colin wondered how soon they would have to submit to new leaders both spiritual and military, once the Romans got their heels dug in. There would be prices to pay for civilisation. The Romans would not stop them practising their religion as long as it did not produce anarchy, but there would be taxes to pay, in tithes of sheep and goats or corn and if you decided to join in rather than be beaten how soon would it be before they took on their religious practises too.

Romans were pagan but they did not specially deify the sun. The Britons would have to learn about all the dozens of Gods and their families and associations and where would their priests be then?

Colin lay back and fell asleep before long, his night without sleep and the wine catching up with him. He woke about mid-afternoon and was aware people were beginning to head off. Yarren was fast asleep beside him and Dai was sitting against his pack, nodding off. Colin felt he would love a swim and signalling to Eiran he walked down towards the river bank in the distance.

There were people from every walk of life, elderly in divans carried by family, children wrapped in shawls across the mothers breast, men carrying young children on their shoulders. It reminded Colin of festivals he had seen on the Ganges, with crowds wading into the water to splash themselves. Colin could see a jetty at the end of the path and a long wooden boat pulled up and tied securely to the posts. Making her way there he could see a veiled woman, golden hair peeping out of her scarf, and men in coloured robes accompanying her on to the boat. He could only assume she was some sort of princess, the colours of her gown were so exotic, saffron and turquoise and as she turned to step into the boat he could see a gold torc upon her wrist. The boat was filled with important looking men and after some bowing and words with the priests they settled themselves on a dais in the boat with an awning to keep the sun off their heads. The boat was rowed by Britons, and it slowly pulled into the stream and was pushed methodically upstream.

Colin was hungry and wanted a wash. They had walked all night and now he felt grumpy that he was not getting food or rest. He walked along the bank following that direction. He did not want to swim where people were washing and no doubt excreting in the water so he followed the boat a little way. There was little current so it was soon out of sight round a wide bend, and having no company Colin stripped right off and sank into the green waters of the river.

It was lush and cool, and cleared his head of the wine. Weeds quite thick waved under his legs but he did not feel unsafe unless of course a great pike were lurking to give him a nasty nip. Unlike modern rivers he did not have to worry he would be swirled into a dangerous weir or culvert nor be damaged by old supermarket trolleys or discarded prams under the water.

In Tewkesbury it had been the dare of all boys to jump off the bridge at the mill into uncertain danger. Usually when drunk or too young to imagine the possibilities, but he had never heard of anyone getting really hurt there. Further along at Shakespeare's boat yard they had dived for coins thrown in before being chased off by local police or watermen, but that was all part of the fun. He floated on his back near the bank and dreamed of his life in Tewkesbury. No activity in Tewkesbury was untouched by the waters; it was a town created by its geography. Three rivers that formed a solitary island that in times of flood was the only part above the waters at that end of town and in the right light, at sundown or early morning the Abbey could be seen as if floating in an opal sea, its huge golden bulk an unimaginable work of Trojans, from time out of mind. For youths that grew up there being in or alongside the brown depths of mighty rivers became the undercurrent of life, whether it was boating, rowing, fishing, cutting reeds or just sitting and admiring it, every person had a personal link with the waters.

On climbing out of the water, Yarren and Dai had followed him and were explaining to people about Colin and his odd habits. Lots of youngsters were gathering round and stared at him as if he were a freak of nature. He had got used to this. Even the Romans treated him as if he were a giant but to see him miraculously lying on his back without sinking or panicking intrigued them.

He reluctantly dried himself on his shirt, put his sweater on and tied his wet shirt behind him. He shouldered his packed goods and made his way back to the spot where the others were still lazing. They roused themselves and began opening some of the foods again as it must now be about four o'clock in the afternoon. He suddenly got the most awful craving for a cheese and pickle sandwich and fantasised about sinking his teeth into thick white bread, soft butter and rich cheddar with a good layer of chunky pickle. He wondered when they would invent vinegar and supposed that was a Roman thing. It would be another sixteen hundred years before the British would discover potatoes and another two hundred before they delighted in chips.

He settled for dried meats and barley cakes, had some mead that Dai had bought and began to think about moving on. Colin realised he had taken for granted that they would wait for him with his alien habits of bathing in rivers and not be annoyed at him delaying their plans, but the celebrations of the shortest day seemed to bring out the mellowness in people's characters. Having a day that lasted 18 hours or so was a blessing indeed. They did not think to tell Colin what they would do next and he was too sleepy to worry. They set off back towards Stonehenge. Colin wanted to stop and look at it more closely. There was lichen on the stones and they looked as old as they had in his day. As he recalled they were probably already four thousand years old then but all seemed to be in place and the curious roofing of rafters and brushwood looked quite new. Perhaps they made it new for every ceremony?

After he had had a good look round they trudged up the gentle slope to the north west and followed the rutted track back over Salisbury plain. He tried to recall anything about Wiltshire and realised he was still assuming he would get back to his own time when he would be able to share all this information. He knew about Salisbury Cathedral and that UFOs were often seen from up here but not much else. As the sun westered in a golden green haze he thanked his own God for keeping him safe so far. It was awful being torn out of his own life but he had made a good job of it even if there was no one to congratulate him. He had seen some fantastic sights and forged a wonderful relationship with Sian, much better than anything he would have had at home with Lesley. Now he was due to become a Dad. He had seen Roman soldiers, witnessed druid festivals, helped to build Britain and supported a community with his fishing and practical skills. It was not all bad.

The sun set and they walked along with the amethyst sky above them. Dai hummed a little song as they walked and the night air after a summer's day was soft on their faces. Star after star came out and that great full moon reappeared later in the night showing them the track in its ghostly glow. The upland gave way to rocky slopes that they skidded down and still trails of people and carts preceded them along the ancient track way. By the next dawn they camped at the foot of the slopes by a small brook, boiled a pan and Yarren did his magic with a bow and arrow. Hare stew and greens and the last of Colin's barley went into the pot. They had bought saffron cakes in the last settlement but had not got back there yet. Colin assumed it was another Roman town but had lost track of where they were. If the Romans were so far advanced he must be in the post Christian era but he had seen no signs of Christianity here. There was a muddling of all things in this part of the country. In Tewkesbury they lived one life. The same food, the same routines, the same goods made, the same religion. Yet only fifty miles away that life was being threatened by a whole new community with different gods and foods, far superior fighting power and knowledge who would wipe away the little tribe he called home one day. They would be driven back into the welsh hills and practice their faith in secret, dwindling to a little people hardly known about three hundred years later. Although apparently welsh, in the next millenium the Welsh were Christians too. How had their culture lasted until his day where wiccans and druids still practiced, albeit under the cynical glance of modern day Britons.

They ate and slept as the sun rose above them. There were trees about this spot and it felt safe and soporific. Birds sang in the trees and Colin saw red squirrels in the branches of the birch trees. The woods were mainly oak, hornbeam and birch but the undergrowth was less here than in the Severn valley, he supposed because it was chalk land, not clay. He loved the feel of dazzling sun through the branches and the feathery fronds of ferns and moss covered stones by the chattering brook. Some red deer came quite close as they snoozed and snuffed the air at these unrecognised beings. The insects buzzed in the blossoms and Colin felt at one with his world.

After another hour's walk they came across a small settlement. They knew about coinage and as soon as Dai showed them the silver coin they rallied around finding barley cakes and lamb stew. Mead was available but Colin did not want to feel dizzy headed anymore. The ceremony had inspired in him a wish to be fit and healthy and he wished he had more interesting food to eat. They did produce some honey cakes which they packed along with a hunk of smoked pork for later meals.

The rest of the day they walked along a green lane, a drovers road going west, which was easy going. Colin recognised it was a different route to that which they had come to Stonehenge. He assumed they were now walking out of Wiltshire back to Gloucestershire again. He thought it funny that he thought of the countryside in random boundaries created in the middle ages which had no relevance to these people but supposed they must have their own mental map to know where they were going. It must be an oral memory of earlier people telling them about the uplands and valleys, to navigate by the sun and moon, otherwise how could they locate the towns and villages. He wondered, as he walked, how far that oral history went. Did they know about towns in the north. Did they know there was somewhere like Scotland? Early saints had lived in the Western Isles and sailed all over the place. They must have some knowledge that the Romans had come from the south, over the channel, but did they have any idea of the type of town Rome would have been at that time?

His thoughts busied his mind and they soon were approaching another walled town in a deep valley ahead. From their viewpoint they could see this was also Roman. Not Cirencester though. He could see the watch towers above the fence and that stone building work was going on inside. As they proceeded down the slope he could see the round huts and blue smoke of a British town outside the fort. Dai approached the nearest camp and spoke with the occupants. There seemed to be some brisk interaction. The occupants were not pleased about the Roman activities and were pointing and complaining, waving arms and making grim faces. They were welcomed and despite their dislike of the Romans they accepted the coin again. It was getting evening and the hearth fires were burning bright, the smell of stews sent their aroma out and enticed the party to join a group of strangers and share a good meal.

They had to sleep on the ground, even those people did not want to share their beds and homes with complete strangers.

Colin had got used to sleeping under the stars and the sky, unpolluted with planes, satellites and light from cities was such an extraordinary arc of millions of stars, those that could not be seen in his world by the naked eye. He easily could understand how peoples at that time paid such attention to the stars and planets. Not only could they see everything at night but they spent so much time lying on their backs looking at them. It was easy to see how they could believe that out there were other worlds occupied by people like themselves, to weave tales of gods and goddesses to name the stars and planets and make a whole dynasty out of the universe. As far as he could recall all societies did this so the sociological effect of the cosmos was inherent in the human mind.

He fell asleep trying to recall the names of Roman gods and how they related to the planets and stars. Uranus, Venus, Jupiter, Mercury, he was soon asleep.

As soon as the sun ceremony was starting they were up and about. Colin had to walk to the nearest river to wash. His clothes needed a good wash too and he was being bothered by lice but did not have the time to start scraping his shirt now. He thought it might be handy to train a bird of some sort, maybe a jackdaw to daily pick the lice out of people's clothing. He could sell it as a service if he could convince people that having insects wriggling in your clothes was abnormal. They fed with the family again and spoke more about the Romans whose fort was comparably large. Colin recalled that in Cirencester he had only been able to get inside because he had been befriended by his Roman guard.

It appeared that ordinary Britons did not go inside the walls. However they did walk down into the river valley where the main river was wide and a bridge being built at the widest and lowest point. It intrigued Colin to see the complex cranes and pulleys the Romans had developed to shift stone. He thought that by this time ancient Rome was already built so buildings such as the Colosseum, palaces for the Emperors and the Pantheon might already be standing. In Britain such sizable buildings would have towered over even the watch towers but he could not recall which towns had had such large buildings. Sure there were circuses and amphitheatres but nothing to compare with Rome. He wondered when bridges like those in southern France were built, Avignon and Nimes and wondered if the rivers in Britain would have such massive sites one day. The bridge on the Fosse Way was over a small river yet the foundations were extraordinary and comprehensive, as if they had no way of making things shabby or temporary.

They walked along the river and looked up the slope to where a huge building site was in process. The Roman guards waved them away as if this project was secret but Colin could see the huge sandy yellow blocks being manoeuvred into walls and culverts and pathways. There was a stream issuing from the site now shuttered in wooden planks and Colin grasped that this was a public bath that was being built over a stream gushing out of the sandstone. Bath! Was this the town of Bath? He only knew it from school trips and family outings. The Georgian town was unrecognisable from the original bathing place with its huge sweeping bridge and weir and amazing walls around the springs, copied from the

Roman original not to mention acres of new built terraces and the Crescent. But he supposed there must have been a time when the original spring was encompassed by the Romans with their sophisticated bath houses. But what of the original shrine used by the Britons? He had a vague recollection that the Romans had shared the well with the Britons but he saw nothing of that here. No wonder the Britons on site were angry and truculent. At least the baths were outside the fort which he assumed would have their own baths for soldiers, rather than the spring which was dedicated to Sulis Minerva.

It would be another two days of brisk walking to get back to Cirencester. The tracks were well trodden but deteriorating in places which meant bogs and marsh had to be traversed and hills were crumbly. Colin could not help thinking how much better it would be when the Romans had paved over all these ancient roadways and made more roads so that all major towns were accessible in hours rather than days both on foot or in carts. The biggest change for local tribes would be the instant influx of new trade. The quantities of food, clothes, wood, tools, animals and most of all knowledge travelling up these roads would transform Britain within half a century to a well run, prestigious country with endless resources and employment and wellbeing, but the traditional life of the little, self supporting villages would be gone forever. Which was best he wondered?

They stopped at another village half way and Dai and Yarren seemed to know people here too. They were given food and shelter in a rather derelict hut overnight which was good as it had started to rain a soft drizzle that would be no fun to sleep in. They were woken at the sun ceremony and soon were on their way north again, climbing gradually towards the South Cotswolds. They passed a swampy river area and then in the distance could see building work on the horizon ahead. Their track was almost petering out in a marshy area but the dust and reflection of sun on cut stone told Colin the Romans were already here. They walked on reluctantly as none of them had felt comfortable in Bath where the Romans were hostile to their presence. Colin hoped he might see his old friend in the work party but these were all strangers. Presumably his old boss was somewhere in the midlands forcing the Fosse Way towards Warwickshire. Most of the workers were Britons again governed by centurions. They glanced up and smiled but dared not stop their work as Colin grinned at them. They had to walk in the ditch alongside for a while and he decided to be friendly waving and saluting in the Roman speech he had learned. The centurions were not much amused at his facetiousness and stared at the tall stranger who was clearly not a Briton. They were asked two or three times if they wanted work but were able to explain they had a mission. It occurred to Colin that if the Romans wanted men to work they could easily have captured them, especially he who had the extra height and strength to be of use to them.

Maybe there were plenty of willing workers here so that was not necessary. People obviously wanted the coin and goodwill of the Romans in this area seeing that the future was inevitable and possibly in their interest. Colin remembered how special he had felt being allowed into the

Roman fort at Cirencester and one day the Britons would be so integrated there would be little difference between them and the romanised Britons. They would inter- marry, their faiths would combine, they would trade and make bonds of friendship. Only when Christianity came along would the rift be irreparable for three hundred years or so.

Once they arrived at Cirencester, now walking along the paved road into town, they sought out old friends they had met at the Bacchanalia holiday and this time it was Colin's turn to pay a silver coin for all their needs. The first time he had tried Roman foods he was not quite sure what he was eating. He felt a bit more relaxed about trying out new dishes. The big difference was the very strong flavours they used, a sort of marmite come anchovy taste to most dishes. And of course the amount of oil that was floating on everything. This repulsed the Britons who were not used to greasy food as their meat was either stewed or it dripped on to the fire. He recalled how they had been astonished when he had collected the dripping to make his Yorkshire puddings. The Romans seemed to like lots of vegetable and salad dishes with plenty of spices and dressings on them as well as a lot of grains. Meat was not half so important as they had such variety of foods to choose from.

Colin asked if he could go into the fort for purchasing foods. As he had been remembered for his height he was also remembered as being in the town before so they agreed he could come in once he had shown them his coin denoting someone who had worked for them. He spent some time with an interpreter persuading them to allow the others in too but in the end only Dai as the oldest was allowed to go in. Colin was amazed at how far they had got with building work in the forum. The flags were all laid into a vast square edged with a pavement and drainage channel. Clearly in England the rainfall was something that had to be taken into account unlike the Mediterranean. He took Dai along the edge of the Forum to see the civic building that he had originally seen as foundations but here were walls and wooden shuttering going up two stories, maybe more. Dai was stunned. Colin could see understanding dawning in this old man about the inevitable changes in his lifestyle; what would happen when they returned to camp in Tewkesbury. Would Dai advise them to start moving into the hills now and settle somewhere remote away from the industrialisation of their land?

Colin took Dai down the lane of the food sellers. Now it was late morning the stalls were all selling wine and portions of food, fruits and meats, greenstuffs and potted jars of preserved foods. Colin was allowed to sample things like olives and sardines in oil, anchovies, pickled nuts and fruits. There were trays of what looked like fried entrails and snails and plenty of oysters and mussels just arrived from the south. He gave those a miss but bought Dai and he some stuffed peppers with grain and mushrooms inside and Dai acknowledged they were good to eat. Their breads were fantastic; of all grains, shapes and sizes, flat breads for scooping up salads and huge rounds of rustic bread for groups to share. He bought himself small pots of transportable foods; olives, pickled eggs, dried mushrooms, sardines in oil, goats cheeses in muslin and a jar of some paste like gentlemens' relish as well as several wheat rolls.

They stayed at Cirencester for two days and Colin thought it must be getting on for July. He had lost track with his calendar stick with all the moves but felt he could count from the Solstice as 21st of June so it was now 27th June.

However Colin felt anxious to be back with Sian before she gave birth he still enjoyed the gravelly river at Cirencester for bathing and the sun was hot on his back when he crawled out as usual surrounded by small boys wanting to learn how to swim. Dai and Yarren spent their time talking with friends, Yarren visiting the ladies of the night again, which Colin refused this time. But he did enjoy glimpsing the sight of rich Romans arriving in carts, their women in sedan chairs with their parasols and slaves from all parts of the world, Asians and Arabs, tiny women with beaded hair and jewels who danced attendance on their rich mistresses, coiffed and perfumed. Like the Britons he could only stand and stare. Companies of centurions would arrive stamping and clattering their armour, their horns and drums announcing their arrival so that the main gate would be flung open so they did not have to break step. He watched the wealthy prostitutes coming and going touting for business among the visitors outside the fort. Presumably they could fleece the Britons as the Romans had set prices in their brothels.

The Roman men posed about in armour and scarlet kilts meeting with their peers in groups around the forum, on stone benches and near the baths to discuss the day's affairs or news from the south. Colin wondered when they last had to fight. He knew the wars with the Gauls were fierce and that parts of Britain fought back but was this before then or after? Had word already gone out that it was pointless fighting back against such unconquerable foes?

Colin's gaze often was drawn to the Fosseway stretching away to the north back to the bridge he built. He wished he could go home but acknowledged Dai, Eiran and Yarren would not have a chance to see their friends again, maybe for life. They did not seem to be going back to work. He wondered why the Romans had not enslaved them but paid them instead. Surely they had the power to take control absolutely but they seemed to want to work alongside with the Britons. He assumed their main goal was transport leading to freight routes for minerals which was why Britain was so important to them. All the time specialists would be out looking for lead and tin and gold and copper in the rocks with a view to mining and transporting them to manufacturing towns where the Romans would benefit from them entirely. By enslaving Britons they would undermine the infrastructure of farming and breeding and would have to feed and clothe slaves whereas by fobbing them off with a few coins they lost nothing. Having battles with local tribesmen just delayed their plans so it was avoided where possible.

Colin knew, having visited lots of Roman sites in the Cotswolds that local chiefs had welcomed them with open arms, took on their ways and manners and enjoyed the Roman lifestyle of villas, hot baths and slaves too. They wanted tiled roofs and underfloor heating and could barter grain with coins and buy luxuries themselves. If the price was tithes to Rome it was worth the price. He recognised the confidence of the Romans around him and the sheer bulk of their numbers and weapons and machinery that could smash a tribe in a day but they still needed subjects to till the land and become carters and farmers and miners and stonemasons, so that harmony was the main goal.

CHAPTER 14

THE RETURN

They ate and slept their fill and once Yarren had had his fill of fun and Dai had commuted with his relatives they set off finally towards Tewkesbury up the valley of the Colne. This was much harder than travelling on roads and Colin wondered if the route via Gloucester would have been quicker if there had been a road built there from Cirencester. Surely as the nearest port Gloucester would have been an early Roman target.

But his friends knew their own world and once they had scrambled up the stream and got into the upper reaches the trees thinned out and they were walking again across the ridge towards Crickley Hill. They stopped for food at mid day and Colin shared his wheat rolls and some fishy paste, but it was not to their liking. Yarren had tickled up a couple of fish from the river and they shared that too. Colin had loaded himself up with little jars and tubs of ceramic which weighed heavily but after carrying fifteen foot poles and then carting limestone paving slabs on to carts his muscles were particularly powerful now and this burden seemed effortless. He also had a flagon of red wine which they did drink and made a merry bunch over the hills with Eiran and Yarren singing a sort of marching song.

Colin had also bought a vial of spicy perfume for Sian, something he had not seen in the village. He knew the journey could only be a couple of days now and was not so anxious as before. She would be about eight months pregnant he guessed. He could not imagine what she would look like. Would she be ill? Could she still miscarry so late? He knew so little about women and babies, no one in his family had had a baby so his knowledge was based on hearsay. He assumed that primitive tribes had ways of helping childbirth otherwise they would not multiply but their diet was so unvaried and limited in winter that the growth of the child could have been damaged these last few months. That said he had never seen a disabled child or a sick one for that matter. Did they have things like measles and mumps then?

Colin was looking forward to improving his eel fishing this year. They were a coarser, meatier fish than river fish and were ideal for feeding a lot of people. He was planning weaving some bigger baskets to ensure they got older eels that could feed eight or ten people each. Gradually they struck down from the crest of Birdlip into the ravine and up the side of Crickley Hill. Lookouts had seen them already and waved as they struggled along the valley bottom. Colin had seen his pole on the top of the hill and in the distance

Leckhampton but he still could not imagine the Romans building a road this way; it had been hard enough in the twentieth century.

They strode up the hill to Crickley and made themselves known to the guards there. There was a keen interest from the villagers and they were taken before their chief and elders to report back on their journey. Colin was left outside and noticed he was being eyed up by a slim girl with grey eyes. She was pretty and rosy looking but Colin felt detached by his status as a married man. She flashed her eyes and spoke invitingly but Colin was not sure how to rebuff her. He shrugged his shoulders and looked sorry. He had not noticed much about young people chatting up each other. There had been one other union in his village and the couple seemed to be always together long before it became acknowledged. Perhaps they were friends from childhood and the families guided them into union. After all, apart from the orgies there were not many people to choose from. He supposed there were about thirty young people in his village and most of them were under fifteen, the older becoming couples soon after that age. He had no idea how old Sian was but assumed about fifteen or sixteen.

Colin waited and waited and eventually the three companions came out looking serious. Presumably what they had said had worried the chiefs here and they were beginning to see their danger. At least the Romans would not want to settle on the high outcrop of Crickley but they might see it as a risk position. They talked for some time after they left and joined their relatives at the same hearth they joined last time. They regaled their hosts with stories of their journey, the solstice and the Romans and there was lots of pointing at Colin. He hoped they were commenting on his quarry skills rather than his behaviour at the Bacchanalia. He slept well having drunk the last of the red wine and laid on his sheepskins under the stars feeling warm enough without covers.

The next day they walked up the ravine and came out looking over the valley of the Chelt. He could see the blue smoke from camp fires but the valley was thick with trees and undergrowth. They walked along forest paths made by the local people and saw charcoal burners in the woods and pigs grazing under the oaks. Very few people were evident and he supposed their camp was deeper in the forest. How different each tribe seemed. Those on Crickley Hill felt quite aggressive and noticeable; these in the valley were shy and retiring. After a lunch by the river Chelt, he guessed about where the town hall would be one day, they made their way up towards Elmley Cross and on to the causeway that was their road home.

The first sign of habitation was the chief's hut and Colin slipped the vial of perfume into his pants. He still smarted from the loss of his hush puppies last time he was interrogated. Colin wondered if any Romans had been up this way before. After all they had been interested in Britain since about 100BC but it took them time to conquer the whole country. From what he had seen of the Chieftan he would relish donning his weapons and setting about armoured Romans. Not that he would have a chance of winning but he would go down in a hail of glory rather than be repressed and compliant.

The outcome of that scenario would be the villagers being punished for their chief's arrogance. Colin winced at the thought of Sian being killed or worse being taken into slavery by Romans and made to work in their brothels. He hurried his footsteps faster towards home.

On reaching the chief's hall they were obliged to enter and give an account of their journey. Eiran as the senior stood forward and spoke for some time detailing their post laying operation and presumably the work they had done for the Romans. The chief leaned forward and looked stern. Clearly he was troubled by hearing about the Romani who could hoist giant stones and bridge rivers and cut swathes of stone flagged roads through marsh and forest alike. He demanded to see what Colin had bought and he showed him the artichokes, fish and paste in the jars. He had eaten all the cakes and given away the vegetables already. The fish and artichokes were not to his liking and he did not search Colin's pants and find the vial. There was nothing the chief wanted from the Romans that his own people could not make or grow. Colin offered the silver coins but again the chief pushed them away disgusted. Eiran had brought an intricate piece of metalwork, inlaid with enamel, that the chief did like the look of. Glass was unknown to the Britons so anything of glass was sought after and rare. They all handed over their little bags of salt but with his fish paste he had forgotten about the salt anyway.

They managed to escape reasonably quickly and it occurred to Colin that what their real mission had been was to spy. How many men? What weapons? What horses and transport? How did they communicate? How fast could they travel? What did they want?

It seemed quite clear to Colin that the one thing the tribe had was the ford over the Severn. He knew there was no other place south of here that you could cross without boats and such a strategic point would be very attractive to the Romans. They seemed to favour dwelling on slopes above rivers; Tewkesbury could not have been a more pleasant prospect but despite this he could recall no Roman ruins here at all. The Cotswolds were covered with villas and roads but Tewkesbury was not famous for remains, but they would certainly bridge the river here one day. Was that the purpose of making the route clear with posts on the hills?

As they rounded the hill of the hall they could see the village camped alongside the water meadows. Its small thatched huts and plumes of blue smoke setting a tranquil scene. Not many people were about on this fine summer evening but Sian's mother as usual was sitting at her doorway with her loom weaving wool into garments and cloaks, Sian's younger brother beside her. She looked, she stopped weaving then looked into the hut and called out. Colin hurried forward but before he could enter the grounds he saw Sian rush from the hut towards him. She looked so fine and bonny! Her belly was large and she swayed as she walked, not running now, her hair a deep chestnut was glowing in the evening sun and her skin looked like gold.

They embraced and kissed and embraced some more whilst Yarren and Eiran caught up with them and the villagers started to come out of their homes and gather round. Eventually Colin pulled away and put his hands on her belly. He gestured "is everything alright" and she beamed yes. Now Colin knew where his heart belonged. They sat out by the fire with all the village listening to Eiran, tales of the Romans and the great town at Cirencester, the road and the bridge and the ceremony at the Solstice. He spoke all night liberally lubricated by mead which Yarren interspersed with comments about the food and girls in Cirencester and the Bacchanalia, Colin assumed.

It was late when they retired and Colin was expected now to sleep in Sian's family home. It was odd, going to bed in someone else's house in full sight of her parents. He had no idea of the protocols of behaviour now but supposed as he was a member of their household. He was also unaware of whether you could have sex with a heavily pregnant woman. Maybe their religion forbade it or something. He spent an uncomfortable night trying to dull his desire while Sian slept beside him.

But how lucky he was. He could not wait for his child to be born and had an inherent faith in their primitive skills to ensure his child was born safely. He had seen other babies born here and the mothers seemed to survive so he did not feel too anxious. He had no idea why women in the twentieth century had problems giving birth so prayed to his own God that Sian would be safe and well. The first day he awoke Sian's father took him by the arm and after the sun ceremony showed him a store of posts-all twelve feet or so long that had been cut in the forest and prepared. There must have been forty at least, from his own experience a considerable amount of work. Her father had led him to an area slightly up the levee towards the sheep fields and pointed to a cleared open space about thirty feet across. Colin realised what was being suggested and he pointed at himself "For me?" Mard nodded vigorously. Somehow Colin was going to have to build his own house!

CHAPTER 15

COMING HOME

Colin had had a good look at Mard's house from the inside. It appeared you dug into the ground using the soil to form a wall on the outside and put the upright posts inside. These were then fastened together with horizontal posts lashed together with twine. The roof was the biggest structure. About twenty four poles were laid from the walls to the centre in a low slope slightly off centre with a sort of garland in the middle. Colin could not see how it was supported, particularly as the weight of the reed thatch when wet would have been huge. Nevertheless that afternoon a party of young men gathered and with Mard guiding them Colin included, they started digging into the soil and throwing it into a wide circle around the edge. Initially it was dry and full of roots but as they got about two feet down the soil became wet and clay like and was harder to dig. On the second day more and more children came to help and this task seemed to be accepted as a community activity. When one tired of the delving in the clay with one pick another took it up. The children jumped and stamped all over the growing mound, compacting it into a clay wall vertical on the inside and sloped outside.

Colin and Sian had been able to sneak away after dusk and before bedtime to reacquaint themselves with each other's bodies. Colin found it hard to contemplate sex with a pregnant woman but Sian's encouragement and direction made it enjoyable and reassured him he was not doing anything to harm the baby. Sian had been delighted and intrigued with the perfume and used it at every occasion much to her family's dislike. Colin worked out that anything foreign was treated with suspicion and was worried he had done something offensive equal to buying her erotic underwear.

On the seventh day after the sun ceremony the priest had appeared from the chief's hall and the village and gathered around Colin's foundations. He was pleased to find they had a sort of blessing ceremony for the building work, the priest chanting and waving bunches of greenery over the site with aromatic oils. Colin and Sian were invited to step into the circle and spontaneously he picked her up in his arms as if carrying her over the threshold and the crowd cheered him on. Once in the centre the priest bad them hold hands and be anointed within the space of their future home. Colin could not but ponder on the difference between that and visiting the register office and the nearest thing to a twentieth century ceremony.

The blessing seemed to encourage people to take part in the building and with the elders giving orders, the hunters and other men and Colin doing the heavy work the vertical poles were all dug in and erected on the first day. Colin was quite fired up himself. He had always been willing to undertake any tasks to be helpful, from collecting wood, working the bellows and walking miles with the hunters but this was the first time he had been doing it for himself. In the evening some of the old men showed him how to split hazel for the wattle. It had to be cut green and Colin could see they would be spending days collecting the right sort of hazel rods for this job. This entailed going to the charcoal burners where the forest was cleared and coppiced to where this year's new shoots were sprouting from the old crowns. In between were the two year old growths, about half an inch thick, which were ideal for the job. With two others and some sharp knives they were able to cut about four lengths from each tree, leaving about half behind to keep the tree growing. After three or four days they seemed to have collected mounds of hazel branches, all long and straight as arrows.

Colin's arms ached and his fingers were sore from removing side branches with his penknife. He was encouraged by the thought that these huts were very sturdy once built and he guessed would last at least fifteen to twenty years so the hard work would be worth it.

Returning from the forest in the evening and seeing his house frame standing proud like a miniature wood henge filled him with satisfaction and excitement. While he was in the forest one of the elders had been fashioning him a door frame. This was built into the mound which was dug away to allow entry at floor level. Colin contemplated how he could make it all more modern. He would like a proper door, a threshold, maybe a doorbell! Even some windows. All the doors in the huts faced roughly south east, the warmest aspect. This meant they faced away from the Ham so the view was the incoming road from the south. Colin would have preferred a view of the Severn but that would have set the door due south west leaving it exposed to the prevailing winds; not a good idea in winter.

Nevertheless he started contemplating a window in that direction. However when he inspected the other huts the earth was so high up round the outside and the roof so low there was no space for a window really so he gave it up. He just wanted to personalise it to his specification. He also noticed the hearths had stone bases, usually a crude pile roughly square shaped. He tried to think where there was an outcrop to easily access stone here. He had worked in the quarry at Cirencester and had got quite a good idea of how to find suitable stone and decided to search around the tut where the Avon cut into the sandstone. He took his antler pick and a smith's hammer that he borrowed and spent half a day scraping and hacking at an area of sandstone. Eventually he had a few pieces of flat stone suitable for his floor.

Once they had gathered enough hazel for the walls there was the difficult task of splitting it. Everyone did a little bit. You needed to have a post stuck in the ground, quite deep. They used the ones around the corral fence to work the hazel so it was split right down the centre. This was a craft that the locals, even children could manage easily but Colin spoilt a few branches before he got the hang of it. The chore seemed to go on for days. Colin had to get some lanolin for his hands they were so cut about and blistered.

As they produced the wattle the women came and collected it and began weaving. They started from the top of the mound, filling in spaces with dead bracken from last year. People came and did a bit between their own jobs, weavers, spinners, children, hunters, elders. All gave a hand at weaving Colin's house. After a fortnight when most of the walls were built Colin decided to thank them all formally at dinner. After they had eaten he stood up with a beaker of cider and made a speech in English. They all laughed at him, unable to understand a word. No one had heard him talking at length in his own language and Colin found it quite strange to be having to think of a format and grammar for the first time in ten months. His neighbours got the drift of his intentions and hailed him with their own toasts.

Sian and Colin slept together with Arna and Mard on the other side of their hut and the children in between. Sometimes Colin woke in the night disturbed by Sian's discomfort trying to find the right position to support her growing child. He lay on his back, without covers as July proved very hot indeed and dreamed of the future. Less and less was he fantasising about getting back to his old life. Village life had little prospects; the same things happened daily, monthly, yearly, but there was a significance and depth about their activities and relationships that made his life seem so much more real and relevant than had working in the bank or even relating to his own family.

For Sian he held the tenderest and most protective love he had ever experienced but with her family, Eiran and Dai and Yarren he felt a strong bond of kinship and trust that seemed to be generated by every gesture of their everyday lives. The fact that all the village were helping him build his home, the priests blessing it, the children stamping down the mound with their bare feet, the tools that were willingly lent, all seemed to validate him as a person of worth and status in their community. The physical work he was doing and his limited diet meant he too was becoming lean and brown and muscular like the village people. His light blue eyes stood out, although he did not know it, like a beacon representing new blood for their offspring, not only to the village but all visitors as well. Unknown to Colin he was a real catch as both father and worker as well as food gatherer, someone the villagers could brag about and show off.

On the fifth day all the walls were in place and the floor stamped into a hard dry surface that was almost flat. At the sun ceremony all but the hunters were present; the sun rose at five and they were off into the woods in search of deer and boar now the young were independent. The oats had already been gathered in by the time Colin had returned but threshing was going on, stacking the oat straw and lots of the women making things out of the new straws. They wove intricate garlands and mats out of flattened straws. Colin wished he could show them how to make straw hats. He had seen it done at a craft fair near Malvern once with a mould for the crown it was quite easy to do. Mostly the straw would be used for bedding in winter and fodder and they made small ricks up behind the village where the wind was sheltered by the small bushes. Colin's hut was on the edge, away from Sian's parents and on rising ground. He tried to assess where it would be in Tewkesbury; perhaps somewhere near the Swan or even his bank! To think all the time he had been sitting at his desk there, deep, deep below were the foundations of his old home, maybe his own bones and those of his wife and child. That if anyone troubled to dig deep enough they might find three flat hearth stones that Colin had just quarried out of the tut. Somewhere between would be the Georgian ruins, the medieval houses, the post Roman settlement and would there be any sign of a Roman building on top of his village? He shuddered to think that at any time they could appear over the horizon, take over and destroy Sian's village and community.

The days were long and hot. Colin got up early to fish, there were no salmon now, but river fish and eels were plentiful. He made his way up the Swilgate, now still a largish river beyond Tewkesbury and full of trout. If they wanted they could eat fish every day.

There was a two day rest in the building project. Twenty four posts had been fitted round the outside and about twelve to make the horizontal purlins at the top. These were all tied in with twine so the structure was quite rigid and solid. He could see how the combined tying in and deep post holes held it all very strongly together with the clay floors and mound outside offering even more solidity. On the third day, by what was apparently an arrangement, all the villagers started on his house after the morning meal; men, boys even the elders all joined in the making of the roof. First they dug three post holes in the centre of the floor where the hearth would be. At the top the three posts came together. Outside was placed a complex circle of woven wattle and it was on this they began to lay the posts from the edge of the walls into the centre. They showed Colin how to knot the twine to tie in each post on the outside with an eave about two feet overhanging the walls. The narrower tops of the posts, now about twelve feet long, were tied into the woven circle in a diagonal pattern. Eventually the twelve ends of the posts held themselves together; they could not sink down because of the angle and the robust tying into the walls. Colin could now see the need for the bracing soil outside. As the weight of the roof pushed the walls outward and the clay pushed inward there was a perfect balance of force. Before midday they had the roof joists on and a smoke hole and all that was required was to take out the three centre posts leaving a hole for the hearth stones to fill in.

Colin and Sian stood inside and hugged each other. She looked really radiant although she was finding it hard to sleep or walk far now. Surely, he thought, she must be ready to give birth any day? How would the house be ready for them?

August was also the month for reed cutting. The hams, now with water at its lowest level were covered in reeds as far as the eye could see. Perfect cover for all the water fowl that were nesting all spring. In the evenings after the heat of the day the villagers went down the hams to the Severn edge and started to methodically cut swathes of reeds. They had two small hand carts on wheels on which they brought the green reeds back and spread them over the ground to dry out.

Colin had been shown how to tie in smaller branches across his joists at varying spacings in order to lay the reeds on top. Even with his weight he could clamber about on the roof. After all wet reeds would weigh far more than he did. The wattle circle in the centre creaked and groaned as he moved from one spar to another but never gave in, so intricately was it constructed to counteract weight placed on any one side.

Two of the men seemed to be the experts at thatching and placed bundles of reeds tied with twigs shaped like hairpins from the outside edge to the centre. Once one layer was on they tied in another layer on top so that it was about two feet thick and lay over the eaves of the walls by two feet. Colin felt bad that he could not help but noted that two or three other houses were having roofs repaired so the need for reeds seemed endless. He was happy to spend all day cutting, knee deep in cool water, and gathering despite the midges and occasional leech. The villagers brought a small pot of charcoal down to the water's edge for this purpose but Colin knew they were harmless unless several were left on for hours. He relished pulling the hand cart himself as his height made it so much easier for him to drag it up the slope and along the ridge from the west side.

By the third week of August the house was completed. Colin thought it had taken four weeks in total. After the roof the villagers showed him how to make daub, with clay, straw and dung from the cattle. The village children were invaluable as they were more than happy to jump about in wet mud for hours. It was messy and long winded but with help the outside of the house took about three days to cover in about two inches of reinforced clay which slowly dried into a brick-like coating that was sheltered under the overhanging roof from rain. Any rain rolled off the reeds onto the mound and away. Colin knew he needed to dig a drainage ditch before winter to take water away from the house but that could wait. Everything was thought of from long experience of living and learning from events for several hundred years. Colin had always wondered about the hole in the roof, when it rained, but when he had stayed with Mard and Arna very little rain came in at all, and although the hole was a smoke hole, there was little smoke inside because in summer the fires were outside and in winter they did not burn wood but charcoal in a raised brazier. It was better than a fire, gave off no sparks and very little smoke, yet you could bake scones on it in minutes and roast meat if you wanted to. In some of the elder's huts he had seen cauldrons on tripods with charcoal burning much of the year. They not only felt the cold but broth was often all they ate and a supply was brought inside if they were unable to sit out with the community.

Once the hut was ready to move into the women brought straw mats they had woven all summer to put on the clay floor and mattresses to lie on. Sian's mother had made a woollen cover to stuff with goose down for their marriage bed and another relative brought a beautifully woven blanket with coloured borders to cover them. Seats were rare and only the elder of the village had a wooden chair to sit on. Colin would have liked a nice armchair for himself but realised this would contravene protocols. Others all sat about on straw pallets or logs round the fire, but he harboured a desire to at least fashion a round, three legged stool at some point. The women weavers all sat on these to work and brought them inside in the evenings. For now it was bliss to sleep with Sian on their own with no relations watching. For Colin this lack of privacy was the most uncomfortable part of his life here. He could tolerate not being able to speak, being cold and doing hard labour but spending all day and all night in close proximity to strangers seemed an assault on his dignity. He had felt so much more comfortable sleeping in the wild with Yarren and Eiran at a distance away.

Everyone brought a present. A bronze bowl with a wooden ladle, straw mats, a brooch for Sian, big earthenware pots and a cauldron on metal rods, goose feathers, plaited containers for carrying food, a crib for the baby. Even the children had woven herbs and wild flowers into garlands to hang indoors and to decorate the interior. While by the fireside Colin twisted lengths of twine and learned how to splice ropes to make longer ones. He knew at times he was going to need endless supplies of string, twine and rope so having a supply hanging on the walls in readiness was a start. Likewise Sian had been busy while he was away making clothes for the baby, tiny blankets and pillows, a liner for the crib that rocked and a fine wool cover for the top. Colin wondered what they did without nappies and hoped all these details were dealt with by the women.

It was soon after they moved in together that Sian went into labour. It was late evening and she started to have cramps and become restless after supper. She wanted to pace up and down and soon Arna and two of the women came for her birthing. Colin was pushed out and wondered what he was supposed to do at night outside. But several of the men joined him, stoked up the fire and kept him company through the long night. He wept when he heard Sian's cries of pain, knowing there was no anaesthetic for her and wept even more when he heard the first cries of his infant. In a few moments he was ushered in to find Sian lying on straw not their bed cradling a tiny boy in fresh woven linen cloth. Her hair was wet with exertion and she looked exhausted but the light in her eyes was worth all the anguish. She showed Colin the baby; it was wholly healthy and pink with dark hair and perfect fingers, toes, and already kicking its feet. Colin was speechless. He insisted on holding his son to the consternation of the women but he needed to prove to himself all this was real and then in a spontaneous gesture rushed outside and held the boy up to the sky. "Thankyou, thank you God for this precious child". There was a glimmer in the east and soon the camp would be waking but for Colin he and his son were the only people in the world.

The women were clearly anxious about Colin removing the baby like that and he quickly restored him to Sian. He was shoo'd out again for them to do whatever needed to be done for the birthing rites. He noticed mounds of blood stained straw that they brought out to burn and something that was taken to where the dogs lay. The baby's cord was kept hanging up in the home for later rituals. The sun was rising and people were stirring. Somehow Colin only wanted to be with Sian or alone not have people talking to him in unintelligible chatter and patting his back. For once he did not care what rituals or sun worship was required for a birth he just needed to be alone for a while.

He walked down to where the jetty was in winter and crossed the new dried out marshes of the ham. Tears rolled down his cheeks which he did not trouble to wipe away. Eventually he fell to his knees, tired, happy and repeatedly thanked God over and over, realising he did believe in a God. Sian was well, the baby was perfect. He felt capable of protecting them and providing for them whatever came along, even the Roman Army. He felt complete, satisfied, as if all at once his life had been worthwhile and with a purpose that was one with the purpose of good.

The sun rose. The tender warmth touched his back and he leaned his hands on the earth and sobbed. Suddenly he heard a familiar sound - church bells and a voice, "Colin, Colin, what are you doing lad?" He hesitated. No one called him Colin now. Again he grasped the earth and closed his eyes. "Come along lad, we've been looking for you all night. What are you doing out here?"

All in a rush of confusion and horror Colin realised the voice was of the twentieth century. He could barely risk opening his eyes but eventually raised his head and began to turn it. "Where are your shoes and socks lad?" said the kindly voice. It was Trevor, his Dad's friend from the Legion and behind him were other voices. Colin turned round to look and what he saw was so appalling he was struck dumb. There were the faces of neighbours of his parents, friends, townsfolk. Beyond was the Abbey Mill, the houses, the Abbey itself. He could not take it in. People were speaking and asking questions but he was mute. One side of his brain was trying to identify what was happening and the other side panicking about Sian. He needed to get back to her, cuddle her and the baby, provide a home, food and protection. Why were all these people between him and his family?

Slowly he was helped up from his kneeling position by kindly outreaching arms. Familiar voices, hands supporting him to walk, tottering back to a town he had left over a year ago.

CHAPTER 16

THREE COINS

Colin was never able to explain anything to his family. He was taken to hospital the next day for a check up. No one could understand how in one day he had become so lean and brown and muscled and so unkempt. Although he used a razor it was still makeshift and his hair was a rough and tufty mess. He had lice and his teeth looked yellow and dirty. There was no sign of his shoes and socks and his jeans were worn to a thread. The assumption was made that he had had a nervous breakdown after Lesley rejected him and this somehow had affected his physical health.

Colin was kept in a psychiatric unit for two days for observation. Although he could not explain anything he could speak and was not hallucinating so he was allowed to go home. His mother brought in fresh clothes and shoes in for him and his old ones were put in a paper parcel to be taken home. It was only when he got home and saw the parcel on the hall table that he thought to look at his clothes.

His mother went to take it from him, "lets get rid of these dear, they're all worn out". He became frantic, "No I need them-let go!" He almost pulled them from his mother's grasp and ran up to his old bedroom. There in the privacy of his old room, he pulled out the linen shirt that Sian had made for him and stitched in green around the neckline. Here in his pocket a length of twine he had been making the night before and-yes- caught in the corner of the pocket three silver coins.

Colin never told anyone. It took him weeks to accept he would never see Sian again and the immensity of the truth was beyond what anyone in his family could bear. He would never see his son again, never know what his name was. He wept with anguish that that night Sian would have been abandoned, husbandless. What would the tribe think of a man who walked out on his wife the day she gave birth! He was mortified. People kept talking about Lesley and asking him how he was but he could tell no one, so fantastic was his story, he knew it would be beyond anyone else's comprehension. They would just think he was completely insane.

As the days went by, gradually he came to terms with his situation, became less tearful each time he thought of Sian, was more and more able to return to his previous lifestyle. He had developed a prodigious liking for fish, which surprised his mother and was fitter than an athlete which surprised his father. His first visit to the pub was weird too. All his friends came down but he looked so different. Not only his physique but those wise eyes, the relaxed gait and air of confidence.

Even when girls that had previously teased him approached he had such an air of self knowledge and experience they began to make eyes at him instead.

Colin went back to work. He often sat in his chair at his desk imagining the layers below the bank and possibly his household hearth stone still lying there.

He wandered along St Mary's lane knowing he was treading the village hearth fire and could remember Yarren and Eiran leading him away to an unknown adventure, the hut he slept in with the hunters and Arna always at her place at her loom, just here, beneath the road. He remembered his days pumping bellows, showing the children new skills, making his first fishing rod and eel traps. He recalled the great love shown to him by Sian and her passionate embraces they had enjoyed all over the scrubby ground that was now the High Street. How could he ever explain these things to ordinary people?

One Sunday he drove down to the Fosse Way. He could not recall where he had worked but knew it was about twenty miles north of Cirencester. There was no longer a bridge or a river here, long dried up no doubt, or diverted in a concrete culvert to build the new roads. The quarry was evident; now within a wood, the scar was still there at the back and he could hear the clang of iron and the hiss of steam as they dismantled the splintered rock.

The following year he attended the Solstice at Stonehenge along with hundreds of hippies. Colin had changed so much in that year. He had become a spiritual person, gentle, broad minded and forgiving. He no longer cared who Lesley was with in London but wished her well. He was no longer bound by social mores and conventions. While he continued to wear a suit and tie to work he afterwards went barefoot on the ham, unshaven, and liked to walk for miles alone with his rucksack, his trusty penknife and his linen shirt. As he walked he liked to jingle in his pocket the three little Roman coins. They never found his hush puppies.

THE END

Printed in the United States
By Bookmasters